EMBER IN TIME SERIES

GUIDE TIME INSIDE

BOOK FOUR

ALSO BY KIM MALAJ

Ember in Time Series
Castle of Teskom
Recover or Yield
Protectors of Time
Guide Time Inside

Who Is Maggie
Twisting Hercules (Spring 2023)

The Old Untold
Failed Book Cover Journals (A-Z)

EMBER IN TIME SERIES

GUIDE TIME INSIDE

BOOK FOUR

KIM MALAJ

Guide Time Inside

ISBN: 9781958502006 Paperback
       9781958502082 Hardcover

Kim Malaj
Haxhaj Nd. 19
Bajze, Albania 4306
www.kimmalaj.com

First Edition: December 12, 2022

For my Art and his supportive, guiding hand while I stumble down the mountain literally and creatively.

N
NW
NE
W
E
SW
SE
S
MONTENEGRO

FORT KELMEND
ALBANIAN ALPS
CASTLE OF TESKOM
BAJZE
LAKE SHKODER

1

"Guide time inside."

"What was that?" Elis asks, unlocking his locker.

"What was what?" Milio asks, sliding on his backpack.

"You said something about time," Elis says. He shoulders his backpack and grabs his skateboard before closing his locker.

"Nah," Milio says, grinning and nodding towards the door. "I was too busy gawking at the cheerleaders to speak." He falls into step beside Elis as they head for the door.

"Hmm," Elis says, pushing the door open. He squints shutting out the glaring sun. "I could have sworn you said something."

"Maybe it was Teuta?" Milio lightly punches Elis's shoulder.

Elis laughs. "Will you ever let that go?"

"You shouted Teuta in the middle of history class," Milio says. "Plus, that's only the third time I've teased you about that."

"Three is enough," Elis says, dragging a finger across his throat. "Bury that next to the insults about 'curly girly' hair."

"Zero puns left, no deal," Milio says. He nods towards the skate park. "Are you heading to the Dome?"

"Not tonight," Elis says, checking his phone. "The twins are coming over."

Milio frowns. "Aren't they like five?"

"Seven," Elis says, pocketing his phone. He drops his skateboard and places his foot firmly in the center.

"Ha, have fun babysitting," Milio says, dropping his skateboard and pushing off.

Elis watches Milio ride away towards the park before he pushes off. He glides in the opposite direction, rolling down the sidewalk and cruising by a few lingering students at the corner.

A lady shouts, "Jace, no stop!"

Elis hops the curb onto the street to dodge the lady chasing her runaway toddler waddling at full speed towards a large dog. The dog licks the little man's face. The toddler bursts into a fit of giggles.

Elis chuckles. He looks over his shoulder to check for oncoming traffic, but flies forward off his board. He stumbles a few steps before he falls to the curb.

Elis stands and inspects his jeans and shirt—a new grass stain and small tear in the jeans.

"Dang it," Elis mumbles, wrenching his board out of the sewage grate. He checks the wheels. One is dinged, and the bracket is loose. "So much for brand new."

Elis plops onto the grass and shrugs off his backpack. He loosens a strap and slides the board through. He adjusts and tightens the board to the backpack before he puts it back on. He hops up and brushes off the grass clinging to his jeans.

Elis checks for traffic before jogging across the street. He sticks to the sidewalks weaving around the afternoon shoppers and students milling about. He nods to a shopkeeper sweeping a stoop on his corner.

The shopkeeper smiles and waves with his broom.

Elis keys in the code to the building and strolls up to the third floor skipping every third step. He pauses outside his door and reaches into the side pocket of his backpack for his key.

"It's open," Anton calls from inside.

Elis pushes the door open and kicks off his shoes. "You're home really early," he says to his dad, glancing at the clock. "It's barely four."

Anton stands from the sofa and gestures towards the dining table. "We need to talk before your cousins arrive."

"What's that important?" Elis asks, holding up his backpack. "Can I at least put this in my room?"

"Sure," Anton says, reaching up to smooth and straighten his tie.

Elis walks to his room and sets his bag and board down in the corner. His laptop is open on his desk.

"Has he been in here snooping?" he mutters before walking back to the dining room. He sits down and Anton sets a bottle of water on the table.

"How was your day?" Anton asks.

"Besides falling off my board on the way home... boring." Elis unscrews the lid and guzzles half the water.

"Is that why I received an email from your teacher today?" Anton asks, pulling out the chair closest to Elis and sitting down.

"What teacher?" Elis asks, folding his arms across his chest.

"Mr. Craven," Anton says.

Elis frowns. "Um, why?"

"According to him," Anton says, "today was the third time this week you have fallen asleep in his class."

Elis shakes his head.

"And that you called out a name last week that disrupted the entire class during an exam." Anton leans forward in his seat. "Care to share your side?"

Elis shrugs.

Anton mocks his shrug. "That isn't exactly descriptive. Try again."

"History is right after lunch, and it's warm." Elis fake yawns and leans forward. "It's like a—nap worthy environment. Plus, it's history."

Anton fights a grin. He manages to keep his expression even and stern. "Never let Kaly hear you say that."

Remembering how the twins' aunt Kaly, spent a good hour explaining the Illyrian era during their last visit to the states, Elis laughs aloud.

"Elis," Anton says, "this is a serious!"

"Dad, it's not like I am failing," Elis says, squashing the laughter.

"That's not the point," Anton says. "Shouting during an exam is not exactly helpful for the other students who may be struggling."

"That only happened once."

"Elis," Anton says.

"And it was that same green-eyed girl I see in my dreams."

"Dreams?" Anton asks, raising an eyebrow.

"I've told you about them." Elis stands. "I'll show you the latest one."

"Show me?" Anton asks.

Elis nods. He jogs to his room and rummages through his backpack before grabbing his sketchbook. He returns to the dining table and turns a few pages before he slides the sketchbook towards Anton. "This is the girl."

Anton stares at the big green eyes set in a heart-shaped face framed by wisps of dark raven hair. He traces the outline of the girl. "It looks real... like a photo."

"It's only a sketch, dad."

"Who is she?"

"Teuta, I think."

Anton shakes his head and pats down the hairs rising on the back of his neck. "And this is from a dream?"

"Dreams." Elis leans forward, pointing out the details of a stone corridor behind the girl. "It's more than that—I feel like I've walked through here."

"Like in person?" Anton asks, meeting his son's eyes.

Elis nods. "You believe me?"

Anton glances down at the drawing. "I do. Maybe it was a memory of a girl you saw while you were visiting Greece during spring break?"

Elis shrugs.

"Kaly mentioned her aunt Xena took you and the twins to a dozen castles during that visit, right?"

Elis nods. "Maybe, you're right."

"And the name you shouted in class?"

"Teuta."

"Ok, so why do you think you shouted her name?" Anton asks, pointing to the girl on the page.

Elis sighs.

"It's not like you to fall asleep in class," Anton says, gently, "and you haven't talked in your sleep since you were six."

Elis's eyes widen. "I used to talk in my sleep?"

"Full conversations," Anton says. "Your mom even searched your room for a phone once because she swore up and down there was someone talking back."

Elis frowns. "I had a phone when I was six?"

Anton laughs. "Absolutely not! You're changing the subject."

Elis shrugs.

"What made you call out and disrupt the class?" Anton asks.

"Teuta was falling," Elis whispers. "I had her, dad, but she let go."

"Had her where?" Anton asks.

"We were climbing down into a cave," Elis says, flipping a page in the sketchbook to a drawing of a dark cave. "She slipped. I reached down and grabbed her hand. I was lifting her up, but she let go."

"And that's what woke you up shouting?" Anton asks.

Elis nods, staring at the sketch. "It felt so real."

Anton reaches over to pat Elis's shoulder. "Does she fall in every dream?"

"No," Elis says, looking up at Anton. "That only happened once, but we were racing down a narrow path and then climbing into a cave."

"We," Anton says, "as in you and this girl, Teuta?"

Elis shakes his head. "Zana, Ora and Emit were there too." He sticks his hands in his hair and lowers his forehead to the edge of the table. "It's nuts, I know."

2

"Emit! Wait until I put the car in park," Danae says, watching her son release his seat belt and reach for the truck's door handle.

"Fine," Emit says, rolling his eyes.

Ora giggles. "She can see everything."

"Yes, little Miss, I can and do." Danae meets Ora's eyes in the rearview mirror and winks. She backs the truck into a spot next to Anton's SUV. The second she slides it in park, Emit swings the door open and jumps out. He grabs his backpack and sprints for the door to the stairs.

"Why is he in such a hurry?" Danae asks Ora, climbing out of the truck.

Ora shrugs on her backpack and swings the door closed. "Something about a new skateboard."

Danae nods. "Ah." She locks the truck and follows Ora up out of the parking garage.

"Is dad's flight landing tonight or in the morning?" Ora asks as they climb the stairs.

"Late tonight," Danae says.

"Will Uncle Vincent be, ok?" Ora asks, stopping at the landing below the apartment.

"Yes," Danae says, kneeling to her level. "It was a routine surgery to repair his bad hip. He may not ride a horse anytime soon, but according to Itra he's already walking Duke twice a day."

Ora nods. "Good. He's my favorite uncle." She leans in close to whisper in Danae's ear. "Don't tell Anton or Leon."

Danae laughs. "You bet." She stands and they climb the last flight of stairs.

"Mom, look!" Emit says, jumping up and down in the open doorway of the apartment. "Elis got a new skateboard!"

Danae laughs as she closes the apartment door behind them. "I can see that."

Ora runs over to Elis. He scoops her up into a huge hug.

"You smell like cotton candy," Elis says, sniffing her hair.

Ora giggles and squirms down.

"Hey Danae," Anton says, walking into the living room.

"Anton," Danae says, hugging him. "Elis has grown at least a foot in the last month. What are you feeding him?"

"Everything under the sun," Anton says, releasing Danae.

Danae laughs. "My days are numbered. Emit already gets up in the middle of the night to raid the fridge."

"I can hear you," Emit says, frowning at Danae.

Danae places her hands on her hips. "Oh?" She bends at the waist to meet his gaze. "So, you can hear me now, but not when I ask you to pick up after yourself or make your bed?"

"Mom," Emit whines.

Danae raises a single eyebrow. "Well?"

Emit turns his back to Danae then folds his arms and ducks his chin.

Anton chuckles.

Danae straightens and smiles. "I should have known uncle characteristics flow directly to nephews." Danae nods at Elis. "Meet Itra Junior." She ruffles her son's hair. "And Leon Junior."

"Stop," Emit says, stepping out of arms reach from Danae.

Ora tugs on Anton's tie. "What's for dinner?"

Anton smiles down at Ora. "Elis mentioned that you three had a plan for dinner tonight, but he wouldn't share that plan with me until you arrived. Care to share it now?"

Ora turns to Elis and Emit.

They nod.

Ora twirls side to side. Her blue dress flutters out. "If we can choose, it is a pizza of our choice... each." She holds up three fingers.

"A whole pizza for each of you?" Anton asks.

"No," Elis says, rolling his eyes. "We just couldn't decide on crust and toppings. Plus, it adds a little variety to our plain old pepperoni and olive thin crust."

"Plain old," Anton says, shaking his head. He looks to Danae.

"Your house, your rules," Danae says. She winks at Ora's grin.

"Pizza party it is," Anton says. "Elis, you can call it in."

"One step ahead of you," Elis says, turning his phone, which is displaying the pizza app to Anton. "Order confirmed and will be delivered in thirty minutes."

"Efficient with ordering pizza," Anton says. "Maybe we can apply that to history class?"

Elis frowns. "Dad."

"Elis."

"Can I see your latest building in Minecraft?" Ora asks Elis.

"Sure."

Danae watches Emit and Ora follow Elis to his room.

"Problem at school?" Danae asks, settling down on the sofa across from Anton.

"Elis fell asleep in history multiple times this week. Plus, he disrupted the class by shouting in the middle of an exam."

"That's not like Elis," Danae says.

Anton looks over his shoulder. The door to Elis's room is open. He leans forward and whispers to Danae, "He's been having a very vivid dream."

"Like the ones he had after we lost Iana?" Danae asks.

"I don't know for sure," Anton says, running a hand through his hair. "But I think I may need to revisit the idea of counseling again."

Danae nods. "It helped him, but it's been over seven years. Any idea what may have triggered it?"

"He's a freshman at a new school," Anton says. "I thought he was adjusting well... until that email from his teacher today."

Danae leans forward. "How are you doing?"

"Busy, but good busy," Anton says, relaxing back on the sofa. "The business is now running with great management, which is taking the load off my plate for a change."

"That's great," Danae says.

"How are you?" Anton asks, looking over his shoulder again. He watches Elis pull Ora up onto his lap to show her something on the screen.

"Hanging in there," Danae says.

"Two weeks without our favorite referee has been a challenge for all three of us. You saw my son's drama display. That's him on a good day. He's been acting out a bit more after Itra extended his stay for another week."

"Those two are attached at the hip most days," Anton says.

"Two peas in a pod," Danae laughs.

"And Ora?" Anton asks.

"She is still little Miss Independent," Danae says. "She can play or draw for hours by herself, but she was really worried about Uncle Vincent."

"She reminds me of Iana," Anton says. "Uncle Vincent and Iana were always so close."

"I catch glimpses of Iana too," Danae says.

"I do envy you and Itra, having one of each," Anton admits. "I never thought I would want a girl or even a second child. But I see how well Elis and Ora interact and..."

"You can borrow Ora anytime." Danae smiles and looks around Anton towards the bedroom door. "She loves spending time with Elis."

Ora giggles when Elis smacks his forehead with the palm of his hand.

Danae chuckles. "Their humor is definitely similar."

Anton smiles. "Along with their artistic side."

"True," Danae says. "I had to buy an additional sketchpad this week for Ora."

Anton's eyebrows shoot up. "Did she bring it with her?"

"I believe so. Why?"

"Elis showed me a few scenes he drew from his dreams," Anton says. "The details are remarkable. And he claims Zana and the twins were with him during one of his dreams."

Danae whispers, "All four of them?"

Anton sighs. "And some girl named Teuta."

The hairs lift from Danae's arms. "Teuta." She vigorously rubs her arms.

"You know someone by that name?" Anton asks.

"We both do," Danae says. She stands. "Can you show me the drawing?"

Anton stands and gestures towards the dining table.

Danae walks to the table and looks down. The sketchpad is still open to the drawing of the dark cave. She traces the outline of the cave.

Anton flips the page back to the drawing of the girl in the stone corridor.

"It's..." Danae takes a step back from the table and raises her hand to her chest.

Anton steps towards her. "Danae?"

"It's happening," Danae whispers. "She's calling the compass to guide time inside."

3

"Zana, it's time to come in!" Kaly shouts from the front porch.

Zana peeks her head out of the treehouse. "Coming!"

Kaly watches Zana duck back inside. She carefully climbs down the ladder nailed to the trunk of the tree.

Leon walks up behind Kaly and slides his hands around her waist.

"What do you think she does up there?" Leon asks, resting his chin on her head.

"Your guess is as good as mine," Kaly says, patting his hands. "I've tried to get an invitation up, but she says no each time."

Leon's laughter rumbles against Kaly's back.

She turns to look up at him. "Have you been invited?"

He winks and kneels to Zana's level as she races towards the porch.

"Catch!" Zana shouts, leaping into Leon's arm. He catches her and swings her around. He sets her down on the porch and groans.

"I believe our days of catch and release may be numbered darlin," Leon says, stretching his side.

"You've been saying that since I was four!" Zana says, scrunching up her nose. "Face it, dad, you'll never give it up."

Kaly chuckles. "Wise young lady we have here."

Leon shrugs. "Truth hurts, literally." He hobbles in behind them.

"Wash up and change your shirt before coming to the table," Kaly says, stopping Zana near the threshold to the kitchen. She drags a finger across Zana's shirt. "What's this?" she asks, rubbing yellow powder between her thumb and finger.

"Guess," Zana says, her green eyes dancing with excitement.

"Dandelion root?"

"Nice job, mom!" Zana says. "Be right back."

Kaly watches her skip down the hall and into her room.

Leon leans against the wall. "She's something else."

"Is she making medicine or potions up there?" Kaly asks, examining the powder.

Leon shrugs. "Itra taught her a few things about plants that could help Vincent heal faster." He steps over to Kaly. "So much like her mother always eager to apply her knowledge."

Kaly leans against Leon. "She's incredible."

Zana bounces out into the hall. "All clean, let's eat!"

"Yes, ma'am," Leon says, standing at attention and saluting her. She freezes mid stride and mirrors his pose. "At ease."

Zana giggles and skips towards the kitchen. They sit at a small wooden table. Kaly dishes out the salad, Leon serves the chicken, and Zana pours the fresh lemonade into the awaiting glasses.

"How was school today?" Kaly asks after swallowing her first bite.

Zana forks a bite of salad. "We had a former Queen for a substitute."

"That's interesting," Kaly says, looking at Leon.

Leon nods. "She took a special interest in Zana today."

"Is that right?" Kaly asks.

Zana smiles and swallows. "Her name was Queen Teuta."

Kaly drops her fork on her plate.

Leon freezes mid chew. "You didn't mention her name on the way home."

"Teuta was in your classroom today?" Kaly asks.

Zana nods. "She left a note in my bag that I am supposed to open with Elis and the twins."

Leon takes a large swig of lemonade. "She knew about Elis and the twins?"

"Of course," Zana says.

Kaly leans back and reaches for her satchel hanging from a hook nearby. She fishes out her phone. She has four missed calls from Danae. She turns her screen towards Leon.

Leon stands patting down his pockets. "I think mine is on the charger." He jogs out of the kitchen to their bedroom.

"Zana," Kaly says. "Can you tell me a little more about what this queen said to the class today?"

"She really only spoke with me. The rest of the class was working on a project."

Leon hurries back into the kitchen. "Kaly, can you meet me in the office?"

"Be right back," Kaly says to Zana, leaving the table.

Zana nods. "Tell Aunt Danae hello!"

Kaly stops and turns. "You knew she called?"

"Ora told me," Zana says. She takes another bite of salad.

Kaly steps into the office and closes the door.

Leon sets his phone on the desk. "Kaly's here."

"Hey, Kaly," Danae says. "Itra's here too."

"Is everything ok?" Kaly asks, looking Leon over.

"I just picked up Itra from the airport," Danae says, "and we are heading back to Anton's apartment. We have a situation here."

"Um, explain," Kaly says.

Danae describes Elis's recurring dream of Teuta with Zana and the twins, his drawings, and how he called Teuta's name out in class.

"Son of a—," Leon whispers.

"And here is the twisty part," Danae says. "Ora has been drawing more the last two weeks. Her drawings are like the scenes Elis drew but from her perspective."

"Do you think we should head to Anton's?" Leon asks.

"Or wait and see what the message says first?" Kaly asks.

"What message?" Itra asks.

"A queeny substitute teacher left a message in Zana's bag today that was meant for Elis, the twins and her to open," Kaly says.

"Oh boy," Danae says. "I can wake the kids and Elis when we get to the apartment."

Leon and Kaly fidget with their gold thumb rings.

"And guys," Itra says. "Vincent kept repeating the phrase, 'You must hide inside to train the guide or time will die' while he was in the post-op unit. The nurse pulled me aside to question his mental status. When he was finally fully awake and talking, he denied ever hearing or saying the phrase." Itra chuckles. "And he accused the nurse of making it all up just to order a full neuro work up."

"Stubborn old man," Leon says.

Kaly flips open a notebook on the desk. "It's been seven years tomorrow since Perseus stole the hourglass."

"I thought once we made it past the six-year mark we were clear of this drama!" Danae says.

"So did we," Kaly says, nodding. "I'll start to work on clearing my schedule. Call us when you have the kids and Anton awake and ready."

Leon pockets his phone and embraces Kaly. She mutters a curse into his chest. "I know, I know," he says. He holds her until she pushes away.

"Go finish dinner and try to act cool," Kaly says, circling her desk. "I'll see what I can push to my teaching assistant and what I will have to reschedule for next week."

Leon shakes his head. "You need to finish eating dinner too."

Kaly ignores him and opens her laptop.

Leon pushes the laptop closed and she glares up at him. "Remember, we said we would tackle this as a united front."

Kaly sighs. "And not divide and conquer."

Leon extends his hand to her. She grips it and squeezes. "Now, take in one deep breath before we open the door."

Kaly straightens and inhales. Then she exhales. "Let's eat."

4

Danae quietly opens the apartment door.

"Dad!" Ora squeaks, running past Danae.

Itra drops his bag and scoops her up. "How's my favorite little Miss doing?"

Ora clings to his neck. "Worried."

Itra draws back to look her over. "Uncle Vincent is doing great."

Ora shakes her head.

"I promise," Itra says, pushing one of her curls behind her ear.

"I'm worried about Elis," Ora says.

Danae picks up Itra's bag and ushers them inside.

All the lights are on. The aroma of coffee wafts out from the kitchen.

Elis and Emit emerge from the hallway.

"Why is everyone awake?" Danae asks, setting down the bag. The coffee pot clicks off with a hiss. "And coffee?"

"Elis said we would need coffee and insisted we remain awake until you two returned," Anton says, setting three mugs and a fresh pot of coffee on the table.

"Emit heard Ember call," Ora says, climbing down from Itra's arms. "I felt it here." She points to her back near her shoulder blade.

"On your birthmark?" Danae asks, drawing back Ora's shirt to inspect the twelve red dots on her right shoulder blade.

Ora nods.

"We know that it's time," Emit says, hugging Itra.

"To return and find the hourglass," Elis says.

"Is the hourglass lost?" Anton asks, filling the third mug.

"Hidden," Itra says, holding on to Emit.

Anton straightens and turns towards the kitchen. "Let me just set this pot back in the kitchen before you explain."

"Let's all have a seat," Danae says, gesturing towards the table. "I'll get Leon and Kaly on the phone."

"Why?" Anton asks, returning to the table.

"Dad," Elis says, pressing a hand on Anton's shoulder. "Have a seat, and I promise you'll understand."

Anton eyes the bottle of whiskey on the small bar in the corner. "Will I need something stronger than coffee?"

"Not yet," Itra says, pulling out a chair for Danae. He circles the table and pulls out a chair for Ora.

Elis sits across from Emit.

Danae rests the phone on the corner of the table and dials Leon.

Kaly's face fills the screen a second later. "Hey guys!"

"Hi!" Danae says. She turns the phone to show Kaly the table. They each wave to Kaly.

"Leon and Zana are here now too." Kaly steps back and shows Leon leaning against the couch next to Zana.

"Anton," Leon says, leaning close to the screen. "We are going to share something with Elis, is that ok?"

Anton nods, scanning the grim lines set on Itra's brow and Danae's frown. "Is it bad news?"

"It's a new message," Kaly says, holding up a gold envelope. "And it may tear open old wounds."

Anton's eyes dart from Elis to a picture of his wife, Iana, on the side table.

Elis reaches over and pats his dad's arm. "It's ok, dad. I promise."

Anton sighs. "Ok."

16

"Zana had a substitute teacher today," Kaly says. "Her name was Queen Teuta."

Elis stands, startling Ora and Anton. "Teuta?"

Kaly nods.

Danae wraps her arm around Ora.

"Teuta gave Zana this message for Elis, Emit and Ora to open together." Kaly turns the envelope over. "Are you ready?"

Zana stands and takes the envelope from Kaly. "It's for us only." She dips her head to the phone. "You can watch me. But I need to read it."

Kaly sits next to Leon.

Danae catches Leon twitch and clench his fist. She glances at Itra. He nods once.

Zana pulls a purple card from the gold envelope. She turns the side with writing towards the phone.

They all lean forward as the card comes into focus. The cursive text is a vibrant red.

Zana turns the message back towards herself. "Before the day is one, Ember's compass will guide time inside to dial the light and retrieve the stone before night. The owl will dress in red. Her power will protect Ember's time."

The group remains silent for several beats before Anton shoves away from the table, rattling the phone. It falls to the hardwood floor.

Danae jumps up to pick up the phone. She taps the screen, but it's dark. The battery had popped loose. She shoves the battery back in place and powers on her phone.

Anton rakes his hands through his hair and bites down on his lower lip.

Ring

Elis's head jerks towards the door. "That's the doorbell."

Anton spins. "It's two in the morning. Who would be here?" He marches to the door and swings it open.

Leon, Kaly and Zana are standing on the landing.

"When the phone disconnected," Kaly says, "we thought..."

"But how?" Anton says. "You were at home in the states!"

Kaly and Leon hold up their thumbs.

Anton notes the matching gold rings. He shakes his head and staggers back away from the door.

"Dad!" Elis races to Anton's side. "It's ok. We know it's hard to comprehend."

"You understand all of this?" Anton asks, studying Elis's face.

"Not exactly," Elis says. "But it's like my dreams. I've seen all of this before."

"Me too," Ora says, stepping between Elis and Anton.

"Well, they can't stand out there all night," Anton says.

Ora grins and runs to the door. "You heard him. Come in!"

Leon scoops up Ora. "How's my favorite niece?"

"I'm your only niece," Ora giggles.

Emit yawns and gets up from the table. "So sleepy."

"It's only eight at home," Zana says after hugging Danae.

Ora pulls back from Leon and looks at Zana. "Great you can take the first watch."

Leon laughs. "First watch?"

"She's coming for us," Ora says, wiggling down from Leon.

"Teuta?" Danae asks.

Zana and Ora nod in unison.

5

Danae pulls out an extra pillow for Zana and a blanket from the linen closet.

Kaly tucks Ora and Zana into the bottom bunk bed across from Elis's bed.

Danae climbs up and checks on Emit on the top bunk before joining Kaly in the hallway.

They stand in the doorway for a few moments.

"Emit is already snoring," Danae whispers, fighting a yawn.

"Come on," Kaly says, tugging Danae's elbow. "Let's have a quick chat with the guys. Hopefully, we can get some shuteye ourselves."

Danae frowns. "Not likely."

"True." Kaly loops her arm around Danae.

They enter the dining room and close the door behind themselves.

"The kids are tucked in," Kaly says.

Anton offers Kaly and Danae glasses with dark liquid.

They accept the drinks and clink the rims before draining the glasses in one smooth gulp.

Danae winces.

Anton, Leon, and Itra tip their glasses to Kaly and Danae and follow their lead. They place their empty glasses on the table.

Kaly coughs. "Scotch or brandy?"

"Scotch," Anton says.

Kaly nods. "Down to business?"

Itra and Danae nod.

"That castle is a damn curse," Leon says. He grips the back of a chair next to Anton.

"Castle?" Anton asks.

"The Castle of Teskom," Danae says, pulling out a chair. "We protect and serve the goddess Ember, but she comes second to our children."

Danae reaches over and touches her gold ring to Anton's palm. He rears back and shakes his head. He closes his eyes and takes in a deep breath as the memories flip through his mind in rapid succession. His eyes flutter open. He frowns.

"You remember everything?" Danae asks.

"That my wife was killed defending that stupid place and that my son and your children were kidnapped?" Anton says, shaking his head. "It's like a wrecking ball to any peace I once had."

Itra circles the table and sits across from Anton. "We've known that this day was coming for a while, but we let our guards down after the sixth year passed with no message."

"That information is not easing the dread I feel," Anton says.

Kaly goes to Leon's side. "Do we circle back to the original plan?"

Danae nods. "I believe it will still be effective. And now that Elis is a little older the risk is even less."

"What are you two talking about?" Anton asks.

"After we returned from the Castle of Teskom," Itra says, "we constructed a few plans to protect the children. One is a ward—"

"A ward," Anton says, lifting an eyebrow. "As in a magic ward?"

"Kind of," Kaly says. "My aunt, Xena, found an ancient text to bless an object to mirror the children. We could see where and when they are."

Anton drags a hand down his face. "Explain."

20

Kaly and Danae pull out matching silver lockets from under their tops.

Danae pops her locket open and shows Anton the mirror inside.

"I only see my face," Anton says.

"Show me Elis," Danae says.

The mirror in the locket fogs and an image of Elis's head resting on a pillow appears.

Anton looks past the locket to Danae. "It's a bird's-eye view over my son's bed. I don't like this!"

"It's just one of the safety measures," Leon says. "We know from experience that Teuta can just show up and take them in the name of Ember without warning."

Danae nods to Itra. He reaches into his pocket and hands Anton a black pouch.

Anton pulls out a silver pocket watch. He clicks it open. He stares at his frowning expression in the mirror on one side and traces the clock face on the other side.

"You will tell us when with that," Danae says. "Try it out."

Anton shakes his head. "How?"

Leon leans over Anton's shoulder. "Show me Zana."

The mirror fogs for a brief second, then shows Zana curled up next to Ora. The clock's long hand moves to three and the minute hand to the four. And today's date appears in the center.

"Where and when," Anton says.

"Yes," Leon says, nodding. "That's part of the offense. We also found a communication device that works across the parallel dimensions."

"Do you recall the gold bracelets we gave to each family member, including the kids?" Danae asks, pushing up her sleeve revealing the bracelet around her wrist. "About two years ago for Christmas."

Anton tugs back his sleeve and inspects the gold links. "They're listening devices?"

"Not exactly," Itra says. "More like thought communication. It's like when we are inside the castle. We can push a thought to another person regardless of where or when they are."

"And with our rings," Kaly says, holding up her thumb, "we can get to the children in a flash."

Anton rests his elbows on the table and balls his hands into fists. "Am I the last to know?" He looks around the table. "Do the kids already know all of this?"

"I think Ora and Emit may have figured out the bracelets," Danae says, grinning, "or its twin telepathy. But no, we haven't shared this information with the twins or Elis."

"Same," Kaly says. "We haven't shared this with Zana either."

Danae reaches a hand across the table and pats Anton's arm. "We made Teuta promise to give us at least a 48-hour window to prepare the kids and ourselves for what may happen."

"And that is only part of the plan," Leon says. "We know that time could freeze in every dimension if Ora and Emit cross under the ember archway."

Anton narrows his eyes and glares at Leon. "Essentially cutting off our offense!"

"Which is why we are leaving for the Castle of Teskom in the next hour," Leon says. "We have to send out the calling cards for the descendants of Mui and Zeus to make preparations for our defense."

"Elis and I are not going anywhere!" Anton says, shaking his head. "You know the sacrifice we've made."

Itra holds up his hands and waves a time out. "I know the loss of my sister." Anton opens his mouth, but Itra holds up a finger. "And I know what we are asking. Regardless, we can either go now and protect them or be left frozen in time. Because Teuta is coming for the kids."

"Why?" Anton asks, standing and leaning forward on the table to go nose to nose with Itra.

Itra doesn't flinch. "Elis is the only one who can find the hourglass, and—"

"Whoa!" Anton shouts.

"Anton, please just let me finish," Itra says.

Anton steps away from the table and shoves his chair in. "He's a teenager, not Indiana Jones."

"It's been a long night," Danae says softly. "Let's just, um, take a break."

Anton leaves the dining room.

They watch him go. Eventually, they hear the bedroom door click shut.

"He'll come around," Danae says.

"We should be ready to go before dawn," Itra says, glancing out the window.

The city below is still dark, with only a few visible streetlights.

"I'll step outside," Kaly says, standing, "and make a call to Pem."

Leon follows Kaly to the front door.

"That did not go well," Itra mutters, turning towards Danae.

"We've stacked the deck without involving Anton," Danae says. "I believe once he hears the facts he'll be on board, but there is no chance of excluding him when it comes to Elis."

Itra nods. "Do you think we should call Uncle Vincent or let him sit this one out?"

"He needs more time to recover," Danae says, fighting a yawn. "And the plan for him was always offense."

"True," Itra says, wrapping an arm around Danae. "But he is the only translator we have."

"I am certain Ember will provide an answer in a pinch," Danae says.

"Ha!" Itra scoffs. He leans in and kisses Danae's forehead. "I wish I had your faith in her."

"It's not faith but spite," Danae says.

Kaly sticks her head back into the dining room. "Are you two ready for some additional news?"

Danae and Itra straighten and lean forward.

Leon steps in and sits across from Itra.

Kaly stands behind Leon. "Xena and Pem received a message three days ago. Teuta has already called in the Protectors of Time and the Zeus allies to assist. The Mui lines are being summoned as we speak. Xena has been reporting back to Pem from inside the castle for the last two days."

"Why didn't they call us?" Danae asks.

"They honestly thought we already knew," Kaly says.

"Knew what?" Anton says from the open doorway.

"That it's time to return to the Castle of Teskom," Kaly says, turning towards Anton. "Teuta kept her promise, and Ember is surrounding us with every possible defensive measure to keep our children safe."

Anton's mouth falls open. The he closes his mouth and swallows, nodding once. "I need to make a call to Nada. She checks in about twice a week. What should I tell her?"

"She already knows about the castle," Itra says.

"Knew about the castle," Kaly says.

"Nada is family," Itra says. "She can handle the truth."

"Fine," Kaly says, holding up her hands. "But she will not like it if she doesn't have all the details."

Danae holds up a hand. "Kaly's right. Nada will ask questions. We don't have answers."

"Fine, we won't tell her," Itra says. "She is my cousin. I'll make the call and try my best to be vague. Is that ok with you Anton?"

"Better you than me," Anton says. "I can't lie to that woman."

Itra rolls his eyes.

"It's almost five," Leon says, checking his watch. "Make it fast. We need to get the kids ready and get out of here before dawn."

"And can you have Nada tell the school Elis will be out?" Anton asks.

"Sure," Itra says, heading to the balcony door. "Get the kids up and bags ready." He hits call and steps out onto the balcony.

Nada answers immediately. "Itra!"

"Hey Nada, sorry to wake you," Itra says.

"What's wrong? Is it Vincent?"

"No, Vincent is great and recovering well. I'm actually back here at Anton's apartment."

"Oh good," Nada says. "So, why the alarming call before the sun?"

"Anton and Elis are going with Leon, Kaly, and my family for an impromptu visit. He wanted to make sure you knew, and Anton asked if you could let the school know Elis will be out the rest of the week."

"Visit?" Nada asks.

"Kaly's aunt, Xena, is visiting up north and asked to see the family, including Elis." Itra grips the rail of the balcony. *Technically, the truth.*

"And you need me to call the school?" Nada asks.

"Yep," Itra says, holding his breath.

"And Anton can't call," Nada says. "Why?"

"By the time we reach Xena, cell range will be spotty, and the school isn't open yet." Itra chews on the inside of his cheek.

"Hmm," Nada says.

"Please," Itra says, turning to look back inside.

The dining room is empty.

"Ok, but if you're lying to me…" Nada says.

"I'm not, thanks so much. Talk soon." Itra hangs up and sighs. "I didn't technically lie." He opens the door, and Ora runs into the room at full speed.

"Dad!" Ora says, crashing into him. "Let's go, we are ready."

He leans over and scoops her up. "Ready for what?"

"To go!" Ora says.

Itra grins.

Ora kisses his cheek.

"Come on you two," Danae says from the doorway.

Itra nods. "As you wish."

Ora wiggles out of his embrace and skips towards Danae. Itra follows and meets Danae's eyes.

"How did Nada take the news?" Danae asks, taking his hand as they join the others in the living room.

"She's suspicious. But only asked a few questions. I managed not to lie. Although, I did keep it vague."

Danae grins and nods. "The kids were standing up and waiting when we opened their door." She picks up her bag.

Itra's eyes widen at once.

"Teuta," Elis says, sliding on his backpack. "She rang her bell."

"The little fairy finally learned some manners," Danae says, opening a portal by chanting the thought: *Protect time, unite to fight. Ember of mine.*

An open door appears next to her.

Emit sprints through the doorway.

"Wait!" Itra shouts, chasing him through.

Danae laughs. "Who's next?"

Ora points and laughs at Anton's slack jaw and wide eyes. "Come on, Uncle Anton." She takes his hand. He shakes his head, and they walk through the opening.

Leon picks up Zana and walks through behind Elis and Kaly.

Danae steps through last and waves her hand. The portal closes behind her.

6

"That will never be normal," Anton says.

Emit slowly spins, taking in the red and purple silk draped walls vaulting up to the large stained-glass dome. He runs the length of the long marble table in the center of the room.

"It's like the circus," Emit says.

"Are there clowns?" Ora says.

Leon laughs and elbows Itra. "Does Teuta count?"

Itra laughs and shakes his head.

Emit points up at the dome with the stained-glass image of a man wearing a cape. "Is that superman?"

Danae looks up and says, "No, I believe that is—"

"Who trespasses here!" Xena exclaims from the open door to the dining hall.

Ora whirls around. "Xena!"

Xena kneels and opens her arms as Ora rushes towards her, Zana close on Ora's heels.

"Hey, Aunt Xena," Kaly says. "Are the others still asleep?"

Xena nods over the heads of Ora and Zana. "I was just out checking on Hermes. He's been flying the perimeter for the last hour looking for any new arrivals."

"Who is Hermes?" Emit asks, skipping towards Xena.

"A friend," Leon says, elbowing Elis in the side. "I believe you had a different name for him."

"Hermy?" Elis asks Leon.

Leon and Danae laugh and point to the caped figure in the dome.

"He's real?" Elis asks.

Leon winks.

Hermes, sporting his signature gold wing shoes and a dark red toga fastened at the shoulders with gold winged pendants, slides into the room behind Xena.

Zana yelps and hides behind Kaly.

Elis points. "I remember you."

"Ah, kid you are nearly as tall as me!" Hermes says, ruffling Elis's hair.

Elis swats his hand away.

Hermes kneels to Emit and Ora's level. "And you two were barely three days old when I last saw you."

Zana peeks out from behind Kaly. "Do you remember me too?"

"Of course," Hermes says. "Who could forget your beautiful emerald eyes?"

Zana giggles and tucks her chin to hide her reddening cheeks.

Hermes bows to Danae. "My Queen."

"Oh, stop that nonsense," Danae says, laughing. "Did you come in with news?"

Hermes straightens and smiles. "Teuta has confirmed all messages have been received, and she requests an audience with the adults in the dining room. I'll stay here with the kids."

"Can he be trusted?" Anton whispers to Itra.

"We are going to be in the next room," Itra says. "I believe Hermes can holler loud enough if something urgent happens."

Hermes nods to Itra before turning to the kids. "Who's hungry?"

"Me!" Ora, Emit and Zana say in unison.

Elis laughs. "Come on, let me show you the coolest trick ever." He waves them over to the table.

They follow Elis and climb into the oversized wooden chairs across from him. "Imagine your favorite breakfast."

An instant later, the table is covered in various plates of pancakes, bacon, biscuits, toast, fruit, eggs, jams, and donuts of every shape and color.

The adults watch the slacked-jawed expressions of Emit, Ora, and Zana.

"Ta da!" Elis says, smiling from ear to ear.

Emit reaches out and pokes a donut. "It's real."

Ora picks up a large strawberry and pops it into her mouth. "Mmm."

Zana looks over at Kaly and Leon. "The castle with a magic chef is real?"

Kaly pinches Leon's arm. "You didn't…?"

Leon laughs and shrugs. "It was either a bedtime story of a magic castle or Green Eggs and Ham for the eighteenth time in a row."

"Eat some eggs and bacon before loading up on donuts," Danae says as Emit stuffs an entire donut in his mouth.

Emit nods covering his mouth with this hand.

Itra points to the open door. "We'll be right through there. Don't leave this room."

Hermes salutes, and the kids hold up their thumbs.

Emit pushes back from the table. "I've never been so full!"

Hermes laughs. "You can eat, kid. I'll give you that." He raises his mug to Emit.

Zana's head is resting on the arm of the chair.

Elis scoots back and stretches. "Zana, are you still with us?"

Zana doesn't stir.

"I think she's asleep," Ora whispers, wiping her mouth with a cloth napkin.

"Why do they call this a 'war room'?" Emit asks, looking at Hermes.

"It is a room designated to gather and discuss strategies for battle, politics, or just dine," Hermes says. "And trust me, when my siblings were all here at once it was like a battle for the last turkey leg."

"And you always lost," a man says, stepping out of the shadows of an open door on the opposite side of the room.

Hermes stands, and the kids turn around to face the tall, dark-haired man marching towards Hermes.

"Leon! Danae!" Hermes shouts. "Teuta!" He glances at the door to the dining hall.

"I know you," Elis says, staring the man down.

"You should." He grins. "We're old friends."

"Perseus," Hermes says. "How did you get in?"

"Oh, flyboy," Perseus says. "Cool your jets."

"I told you not to call me that!"

"I'm family," Perseus says, waving towards the door. "My bloodline opens any door here since the Zeus family has now been restored as guardians."

Hermes shakes his head. "Ember banned you for life after you stole the hourglass from the vault." He steps between Perseus and the table.

"More like secured the hourglass for her," Perseus says. He winks at Hermes.

Hermes puts his hand behind his back. He waves to Elis, pointing across the table.

Elis stands quickly and rounds the table.

"Where do you think you're going?" Perseus asks.

Elis steps between the table and the chairs with his cousins.

Emit and Ora stand and duck behind him.

Zana stirs and sits up, eyes blinking open. "Who are you?" she asks.

"Ah, the changeling," Perseus says and winks at her.

Zana frowns.

"Why are you here?" Hermes asks, blocking Perseus's view of the children.

"To retrieve the compass and time for Ember," Perseus says.

"Why would Ember send you?" Hermes pokes Perseus in the chest.

"Because I know where to look."

Hermes smirks. "Doubt that."

"Oh?" Perseus raises a single eyebrow.

"Leave now," Hermes says, pointing towards the dining hall.

"And walk into that drama fest of worried adults." He reaches inside the pocket of his tight tunic. "No, thank you." He pulls out a small envelope. "Plus, I came with a message." He holds it up.

Hermes sees his name written across the front. He reaches for it, but Perseus pulls it out of his reach.

"I'll trade you the message for time and the compass," Perseus says.

"No deal," Hermes says.

Perseus nods. "Your choice." He pockets the envelope. "Disobey her orders and see how well that turns out. He grips the back of the chair next to Hermes.

"I'm here on her orders."

"Things change," Perseus says. He suddenly lifts the chair by its back and swings it at Hermes.

Hermes crashes to the floor.

Perseus leaps across the table.

Ora runs for the door to the dining hall, but Perseus scoops her up by the waist and turns towards the others.

Hermes pushes the weight of the chair off his chest and gets to his feet. "Perseus! Put her down!"

Elis runs towards Perseus, but he is lifted in the air and slams against the wall, frozen in place a foot off the floor.

"Elis!" Ora shouts, struggling to break free from Perseus's grip.

Emit punches Perseus's back. "Let her go!"

Elis attempts to move but can't. *Why am I frozen?*

"Remember," Perseus says, "I'm here on behalf of Ember." He points to Zana. "Did you get her message?"

Zana nods. "But you're not the owl."

"Dear child," Perseus says, tilting his head towards the door he entered. "Did you think I would come here alone?"

A tall, dark, curvaceous woman leans against the frame. Her ebony curls are pulled to one side. They hang past her waist and hide one of her hands.

Hermes's eyes bulge. "Andromeda!" He starts around the table but loses gravity and is launched to the wall next to Elis. His feet dangle and his mouth feels glued shut.

"Before the day is one," she sings and points to Elis. "Ember's compass will guide time inside to dial the light and retrieve the stone before night." She flutters her red tunic. "The owl will dress in red. Her power will protect Ember's time." She points to Emit.

Elis attempts to move his jaw and utters a muffled scream behind sealed lips.

Zana meets Elis's eyes.

"Run!" Elis mutters behind his clenched teeth.

"Tsk, tsk," Perseus says, wagging his finger at Zana and Emit. "If anyone makes a run for it or another sound, Andromeda will muzzle and freeze you as well." He nods to the corner near the dark antique wardrobe.

Andromeda saunters to the corner and opens it.

"We need a little help in here," Hermes mentally shouts, pushing his thoughts towards the adults in the dining room. He glares towards the door. *"Like now!"* He glances around the room. *"Why aren't they bursting through that door?"*

"I can hear you," Elis answers in thought. *"I remember this from my time here before."*

"We're normally all linked with thought communication," Hermes answers. *"It was working before you arrived. I don't know why they aren't responding!"*

Five red and purple feathered cloaks float out of the wardrobe. Two cloaks hover in front of Hermes and Elis. And three float over to Perseus and the children.

Emit stops mid punch to watch the cloaks glide through the air. His jaw gapes wide open.

"Like an owl, we must fly," Perseus says.

"We don't have wings," Emit says, reaching out to stroke the feathers. "It's silky."

A shadow falls over the room.

Perseus looks up at the dome as the stained-glass image of Athena is pulled out of the surrounding images. A man's head sticks through the hole. His silhouette is dark, backlit from the sun. "Send the smallest one first."

Hermes shifts his gaze to assess the man but can't identify the newest intruder. *"Leon, Danae, anybody!"*

"Allow me to repeat myself: if anyone makes a run for it or another sound," Perseus says. "Andromeda can muzzle you three just like she has muzzled Hermes and Elis."

Emit purses his lips and flares his little nose.

Zana jumps out of her chair and places a hand on Emit's shoulder.

Two of the cloaks fall close to them.

"Turn around and stretch your arms out," Perseus says, pointing to Emit and Zana with this free hand. He makes a twirling gesture with one finger.

They away from the cloaks and extend their arms.

The cloaks fall onto their backs disappearing into their clothes.

Emit looks over his shoulder and frowns.

Andromeda walks towards Zana.

Hermes grunts. *"Itra, Xena, Teuta!"*

"Take my hand," Andromeda says, holding out her hand to Zana.

Zana shakes her head. "I don't know you."

"Fine," Andromeda says, revealing the hand that had been hidden under her hair. The jewels on her rings sparkle and dance around the room. She lets her wrist fall loose, and she flaps her hand.

Zana's feet lift from the floor. "Stop!" She waves her arms around and kicks.

Emit tugs on her legs.

Andromeda stills her hand, closes her index finger to her thumb, and flips her hand palm up.

Zana spins with her back to the floor.

Emit loses his grip.

Zana flies up towards the opening.

Emit opens his mouth to shout, but Andromeda clamps her hand over his mouth.

The man at the opening catches Zana and she disappears out of view.

"Remember, not a word," Andromeda whispers into Emit's ear.

Emit sniffles and nods.

She shoves him up and he flails around trying to fly back down. But the man reaches for him and pulls him through the opening.

Ora twists and attempts to bite Perseus's arm, but he turns her back to Andromeda. The feathered cloak melds into Ora's dress and a purple halo of light appears around Ora.

"Ora, if you can hear me," Hermes says, *"your cloak can shield you from sight."*

Ora looks over at Hermes.

Andromeda steps back.

The purple light fades.

"What was that?" Andromeda asks, guiding Ora up to the man in the opening.

"I'm not sure," Perseus says, turning for Hermes and Elis. He shoves the cloaks forward onto them and the cloaks vanish.

Andromeda turns her attention towards Elis and Hermes.

"She is going to guide your flight out of here," Perseus says. "The same rules apply. You make a peep or try to fly away. I'll hand Ora over to Chronos. Blink once if you understand."

Elis blinks immediately.

Hermes glares at Perseus for three full seconds before he blinks.

"Great," Perseus says, nodding to Andromeda. "Release them and fly them out like we planned. I'll need to make a bit more of a scene to throw off the adults."

Andromeda laughs. She waves her hand and releases Hermes and Elis. Once they are safely out of the war room, she nods once to Perseus and flies up through the hole in the dome.

Perseus tosses a few chairs over and shoves plates to the floor. He takes the remaining cloaks from the wardrobe, runs for the stairs, and jogs up to the first landing. He presses on a stone in one of the walls—it clicks, and he pushes against the wall to

34

its right. The entire wall swings in, revealing a hidden passage. He ducks in and swings the wall back into place.

He taps his ring finger on a small, round stone and tosses it up. It hovers above him, glowing brightly. The new light adjusts to the space. He moves forward five paces, turns right, walks another twenty paces and stops. He kneels next to a large open chest. He shoves the cloaks inside, gently closes the lid, locks it, and pockets the iron key.

Perseus pulls on a dangling rope, and the floor lifts up revealing an old iron ladder. He squeezes his large frame into the tiny hole and climbs down. His feet find solid ground, and he pulls on a wooden lever, lowering the floor back into place. He turns and follows a pinhole of light. He bends lower to avoid the stalagmites overhead. The light expands from the size of a dime to the size of a small window. He holds out his hand, and the light stone dims and drops into his open palm.

"How am I supposed to fit through there?" Perseus asks, examining a fallen rock covering most of the narrow passage. He pushes against it—it budges an inch, but the rock remains wedged in the path. He sticks his arm in the space above it and gets stuck just past his elbow.

"Ember, a little help here," Perseus mutters, dust flying as he yanks his arm out. He holds his nose attempting to squash a sneeze. The sensation dissipates and he sighs. He turns his back to the rock, leans back, and squats down attempting to move it again.

The rock doesn't budge.

Perseus grunts and throws his light stone back up into the air. He navigates away from the stone, back the way he came.

After several minutes, he turns around. The rock blocking his path is still only a foot away.

"No." Perseus turns in a slow circle. He throws back his head and balls his fists. "Ember!"

7

In the dining room, Anton takes in the vibrant purple walls. "I liked it better yellow," he says to the others.

"It's hard to accept change," Teuta says, appearing next to Anton. Her dark raven hair is swept up in a high ponytail and she blinks her wide set green eyes up at Anton.

He leaps back. "Why! Seriously!" He places a hand on his chest.

Teuta jingles the bell hanging around her neck.

Leon rolls his eyes. "And we thought she had manners."

Itra just laughs and places a hand on Anton's shoulder. "Junior hates the color too," he says.

A man's voice says, "Hate is a strong word."

Itra turns and cowers at the height of Junior towering over him. "Where did you come from?"

Junior smirks. "That's a need to know."

Itra looks him over. His hair is messy. Itra leans in, plucking a long raven hair from his tunic. He looks at Teuta, who immediately looks away. "Ha!" he says to Junior. "You've been… busy. Have you two kissed and made up or what?"

Junior takes a step back. "Two who?"

Leon laughs.

Anton leans across the table. "I'm lost." He glances at Teuta's reddening cheeks.

"Teuta and Jun—," Leon says.

"Enough," Junior says, walking to the chair at the head of the table. "We have business, not gossip to discuss."

Teuta's red dress flutters out as she marches towards the other end of the table. "Let's begin." She waves her hand.

The hall falls dark except for a single beam of light from the glass dome highlighting an image of the hourglass Perseus stole from the vault.

"Seven years ago, we discovered that the mural on the floor is the prophecy of the four dimensions merging into one new world."

The beam of light expands over the dining hall.

Anton turns and looks at the tile mosaic. He scans the outline of a circle, divided in four equal quadrants, draining into a dark hole in the center.

The image of the hourglass rises from the table and tips over.

"A day will come when this world is one," Teuta says. "A divine bride will lead the guide inside to begin again. He must tip the end. Four worlds will bend and fold to derive a world untold."

The light of the hall turns a shade of blue and the hourglass spins exposing three symbols etched in the glass.

Xena points and says, "The three symbols translate to begin again or tip the end and the phrase bind my line with thine time."

"Who is 'my line'?" Anton asks, shifting in his chair.

"After some research…" Xena says, looking over at Kaly. Kaly nods. "We believe it is Zana."

Kaly leans forward. "We believe this because of Zana's lineage to Ember through Prende. There is also the message Enyo received from the Anubis scale." She balls her hands into fists and places one on top of the other. "Stack the stone against your own. A compass to guide is near inside. To begin again or tip the end. You must decide."

The image of the hourglass fades to a gold scale tipped to one side with the ruby stone in pointed gold resting in the higher saucer. A round smooth stone appears in the other saucer.

"The urtar stone is the key to balance," Junior says.

"Seven years ago," Teuta says. "Princess Danae hid the hourglass with the urtar stone inside the sundial located in the center of the City of Time."

Danae nods. "Right, we knew this. Has this changed?"

Teuta shifts her eyes to Junior. He gives a slight nod.

"No," Teuta says. "The reason you were summoned here today was because the future cavern collapsed four days ago."

"Was anyone hurt?" Danae asks.

"Yes," Teuta says. "Ana was inside when—"

"Ana?" Anton says, standing and searching the room. "She's here?"

"She's sedated to aid in her recovery," Junior says. "My sister Dita arrived a few hours after the incident thanks to Teuta's quick message."

Kaly turns to Xena. "Did Pem know about this?"

"No," Xena says, frowning. "This is the first time I've heard anything about it."

"But you've been here for days, right?" Itra asks.

"Yes," Xena says, glaring at Teuta.

Teuta shrugs. "I told you the future cavern was off limits."

"Not exactly," Xena says. "I remember heading to the future cavern, and you cut me off to run a message to Hermes."

"Ana has the gift of prophecy," Leon says. "This collapse must have been intentional."

"Because we're now flying blind," Danae says.

"If someone was close enough to destroy the cavern, are the kids even safe here?" Kaly asks, scooting back from the table.

"I completed a full reset," Junior says, "just to be sure. But there are fissures in the present cavern suggesting that the collapse may have happened naturally."

Teuta nods. "An earthquake registered just north of here two hours before the collapse."

"Was Ana here at the castle alone?" Itra asks.

"Yes," Teuta says. "She arrived on her own stating she had a series of visions that Chronos was coming and wanted to confirm her visions using the future cavern."

"And where were you when the collapse occurred?" Leon asks, tilting his head towards Teuta.

"In my suite," Teuta says. "It was just after midnight when Ember sent me to the rubble. Ana was pinned under a large rock but she was still conscious. She kept repeating, 'He is near, check the rear,' and I asked her if 'he' was Chronos. She never confirmed or denied this, just repeated the phrase until she passed out."

"Why would Ember leave Ana down there?" Itra asks, shaking his head.

"I've been asking myself that same question," Dita says from the door to the conservatory.

All eyes turn towards Dita. She walks towards the table.

"Ana," Dita says, "is medically cleared, all her injuries are healed." She pulls out a chair and sits. "But she still has not regained consciousness. I've weaned all sedation. I'm questioning if this may be a prevention tactic to keep her from speaking about what she saw before the cavern collapsed."

"Does she have a head injury?" Xena asks.

"No," Dita says. "I've scanned her entire body for any anomalies, and everything appears perfect." She shakes her head. "Which is why I believe that her ability to wake is being suppressed by something external."

All eyes focus on Teuta.

Teuta holds up her hands. "I don't have any answers. Just the same questions."

"First Iana dies and now her doppelgänger is crushed in Ember's cavern," Anton mutters. "Who's next?"

Danae and Kaly stand at once.

Anton jumps up. "The kids?"

The three of them sprint towards the war room.

They crash through the door all at once.

Anton falls on his knees. "Elis!"

"Zana!" Kaly shouts.

"They're gone," Danae cries.

Leon, Itra, and Xena step inside the chaotic scene.

Xena circles the table stepping over the plates of food tossed on the floor. She checks the large wardrobe in the corner.

"The feathered cloaks are gone," Xena says, slowly turning to face the others.

The morning breeze rattles the silk-lined walls.

Itra and Leon point up to the opening in the stained-glass dome.

8

Leon calls his staff and points the glowing end at Teuta's chest. "Where is Ember? Why would she take the kids?"

Teuta vanishes and appears five steps away. "She's here, I think." She points to the ember staff and to Leon's forearm. "Otherwise, your ink would vanish, and your gifts would no longer work."

"Explain," Danae says.

"The castle is Ember," Teuta says. "Ember is the castle. They are part of one unique matter."

"And the children?" Kaly asks, waving her hands to the room. The sunlight glints off her gold bracelet. She slows her motion.

"She wouldn't hurt them," Junior says, joining the group. "She may have hidden them from whoever did this damage." He picks up a plate and rights a chair. "Let's start a search of the suites and meet back here."

"They should be able to hear us!" Kaly says, holding up her bracelet. "We didn't have time to teach them how—"

"No need," Anton says, holding up the pocket watch. He turns towards Kaly and Danae.

They pull out their lockets.

"Show me our children," Kaly says.

The mirrors fog. The three of them gasp in unison. Itra and Leon lean forward.

Ora is hand in hand with a tall, cloaked figure walking her through an ember archway. The view pans back and shows Emit and Elis struggling with three men, dressed in tan tunics and sandals. They push the boys through another archway.

Anton shakes the pocket watch. "The clock is stuck at twelve and the date just zeroed out."

Kaly turns to Xena. "How do you fix it?"

"Um," Xena says, shaking her head. "Try focusing on one child at a time."

"Show me Zana," Kaly says.

Zana tumbles head over heels through the air towards the lake. The view widens and shows Hermes fighting to break free of a large man holding his legs.

"Oh!" Anton shouts. He holds up the watch. "She's here and now, our time."

Teuta vanishes and appears with Zana in less than a second.

Zana's mouth is still open in a scream. Her wavy brown hair is windblown in every direction. She closes her mouth when her feet hit the floor.

Kaly lunges towards Zana. "Zana, baby, are you ok?" She cups Zana's chin while she looks her over.

Leon releases his staff and hugs them both.

"I'm ok, but Ora and Emit," Zana says. Her bottom lip quivers. "Elis..."

Danae turns to Teuta. "Why are you just standing there? Go get them!"

"I'm trying," Teuta whispers, staring at the floor.

"What?" Itra asks, looking her up and down. "Try harder!"

"They've stopped time," Teuta says, looking up. "I don't know how. Ember is my compass and without her guidance I'm stuck."

Leon takes a step away from Kaly and Zana, calls his staff and double taps it on the floor. A translucent scythe replaces the ember glow. He levels the curve of the blade around Teuta's tiny neck.

Teuta sharply inhales. She attempts to portal but can't move.

Junior steps towards Leon but stops once he meets Leon's glare.

"Easy," Junior says, stepping back holding up both hands.

"Show me Ora," Anton says, stepping between Danae and Itra.

Ora's heart-shaped face fills the mirror.

The focus blurs and pans out. Ora is sitting on a boulder facing a woman, whose hood falls back exposing her warm, dark complexion and long, dark hair.

Junior looks over Anton's shoulder. "That looks like Andromeda, Perseus's wife."

Kaly turns towards Junior. "The Ethiopian princess he rescued from a rock?"

"Yes," Teuta says without tearing her eyes away from the scythe.

Danae points to the face of the watch. The shorter hour hand spins back to the twelve and the minute doesn't budge. The date rolls back to zeros.

"What's happening?" Anton asks.

"Time is frozen," Teuta says.

"Show me Elis," Anton says.

The mirror blurs away from Andromeda's face to Elis protecting Emit from three men charging towards them.

The clockface dials to 21/06/18 and stops.

"June 2018?" Itra asks.

"I don't think so," Danae says, pointing to the stone wall and dirt path behind Elis and Emit. "I think it's 18 BC."

"Leon," Itra says. "Do you think you could slice a window to them?"

Leon nods. He slowly raises the scythe releasing Teuta. She runs a hand over her neck. Anton turns the mirror towards Leon.

The group steps back as Leon makes four quick swipes through the air with his scythe. An opaque square appears and shimmers. It clears, revealing Elis and Emit. They're cornered with their backs pressed against a stone wall.

"Stay back!" Elis shouts at the approaching men, holding Emit's hand.

Danae and Leon make eye contact before chanting in unison, "Protect time, unite to fight. Ember of mine."

The square opens to a door, and Danae and Leon rush through.

"No!" Itra reaches for Danae, but his hand finds only air as the door vanishes. "Get it back!"

Xena places a firm hand on Itra's shoulder. "Let's divide and conquer."

Itra mutters a curse.

"We know Ora and Andromeda are alone just across one of the ember archways." Xena points towards the dining hall. "The communist dimension doesn't have a boulder similar to that on the other side—that leaves us with only two to check." She turns towards Teuta. "You've crossed all three ember archways. Which one has a boulder low and large enough for her to sit on?"

"Revolutionary," Ana says from the open door leaning against Dita.

"Ana," Anton says, rushing towards her. "Are you ok?"

"I've been better," Ana says, embracing Anton. "Elis?"

"Taken along with the others," Anton says.

"Chronos is coming," Ana says.

"When?" Teuta asks.

"Soon," Ana whispers.

Itra turns his focus to Ana. "Can you show me where the boulder is?"

"Show us both," Xena says, pointing to Itra and herself.

Ana nods. "You'll need a cloak. It's not your world."

Itra shakes his head. "They're gone."

Zana holds up her hand. "The feathered ones?"

Kaly nods.

Zana smiles. "I have one on!"

"Great," Kaly says. "Turn around and extend your arms."

Zana turns and lifts her arms.

The cloak appears and hovers just behind her.

Itra turns and extends his arms. The cloak turns and drapes over him, vanishing on contact. He looks over his shoulder. "Let's go!"

Dita looks at Junior. "Brother, are you coming?"

Junior glances at Teuta.

Teuta nods.

Dita rolls her eyes. "Let's go. Andromeda won't stay put for long."

"She can fly," Kaly says, "if the legends are true. I'll stay here with Zana and Anton."

Itra nods. "Head up to the tower. We need eyes in the sky just in case she takes off before we can get to Ora."

Teuta attempts to move as the others race through the dining hall. She grunts when her feet remain glued to the floor. "I can't move! Ember?"

9

"Mom!" Emit shouts.

One man looks back and sees Leon's scythe swinging towards him. He blocks the assault with the blade of his sword. He wobbles back buckling under Leon's push.

The clash of the blades distracts the other two men. They fan out and raise their swords.

Danae uses the distraction to circle the men. "Back up," she whispers, pushing Elis and Emit behind her.

A second man lunges at Leon, swinging his sword towards his head.

Leon kicks the first man hard in the chest and he staggers back, freeing Leon's blade to swipe down on the second man's arm.

The man's sword clatters to the ground still in his grip, and his knees buckle as the blood rushes out. He falls face first into the dirt at Leon's feet.

Leon doesn't blink and double taps his staff back to the warm ember glow. "Burn." He taps the ember glow to the ground. The two remaining men turn to flee, but a circle of fire erupts, surrounding them.

"Danae, take them back now!" Leon says, stepping over the fallen man.

Danae nods, fighting back the urge to vomit. "Protect time, unite to fight, Ember of mine." She glances around. "Where is the freaking door?"

Elis taps Danae on the shoulder.

She turns to find Emit and Elis standing inside a shimmering doorway. "Oh, thank goodness." She turns back to Leon. "Let's go!"

Leon walks backward keeping the men in his line of sight. Danae tugs on his arm once he's close and the four of them collide through the open door.

It slams shut as they stumble into the dining hall of the Castle of Teskom.

Danae falls to her knees. "Emit, are you hurt?"

Emit shakes his head as the color returns to his pale face, which is dripping with fallen tears.

Danae pulls him in for a tight hug.

Leon releases his staff and puts a hand on Elis's shoulder. "Thanks, kid, you did great protecting Emit. Are you ok?"

"That was terrifying," Elis says. "Did you just kill those men?"

"I can't say the man missing his arm will make it, but the other two will be fine."

"Zana was taken by another man," Elis says. "Hermes and I tried to stop him."

"And Ora was taken by that witch, Android," Emit says, pushing back from Danae.

"Andromeda," Elis says with a small smile.

"We got Zana back," Danae says, looking around the vacant and quiet dining hall. "But where are they now?"

Leon looks around. He pushes his thoughts towards his wife. *"Kaly, where are you?"*

"In the tower off the main entrance with Zana and Anton," Kaly answers. *"Did you get the boys?"*

"Yes," Leon says. "Kaly, Zana, and Anton are in one of the towers."

"And Itra?" Danae asks.

"Where are the others?" Leon asks Kaly, waving Elis towards the door to the conservatory.

"They went after Ora," Kaly answers.

"Itra is finding Ora, sis," Leon says. "Elis, can you tell me what happened on the way up to your dad?"

Elis nods.

"Danae, are you good to stay and wait here for the others?" Leon asks.

"We're good," Danae says, pulling out two chairs. "Emit and I are going to have a cup of hot chocolate with extra marshmallows."

Leon taps his temple. "Just a thought away." Then he leads Elis out to the conservatory.

Emit whirls and climbs into the chair. A steaming mug stacked high with white fluff arrives on the table.

"Sip slowly," Danae says, sitting down next to him. "Can you tell me what happened and who took you?"

Emit swallows. "Hermes was mad! He said that man was banned from here."

"He's right to be mad," Danae says. "Perseus stole something from the vault."

"But Persy said he was here because of Ember," Emit says.

Danae shifts in her chair. "And the woman?"

"She sang the message Zana received from Teuta," Emit says, taking another loud sip from the mug.

"Teuta," Danae says, pushing out her gift of perception. *Nine souls in the castle, hmm. Maybe Dita stayed back with Ana.*

Emit sets the empty mug on the table bringing Danae's focus back to him.

"Why did you call her a witch?" Danae asks Emit.

"She had powers that she used to hold Elis and Hermes against the wall." Emit twirls his hand. "And she was wearing a lot of rings and bracelets on one hand. Like the bad guy who snaps."

"Thanos?" Danae smirks and nods. The decision to prevent the kids from watching anything superhero related had proved to be a losing battle—especially while Itra was away.

48

"And the men who were chasing you?" Danae asks.

"Friends of the witch," Emit says, jumping out of the chair. "Where's the bathroom?"

Danae takes him to a door adjacent to the conservatory. She pushes it open to reveal a long, stone corridor, full of portraits from the previous and current bloodlines. She activates her light stone with a tap and a toss.

Emit points up. "How did you do that?"

"Magic." Danae winks.

Emit skips ahead to the open door on the left.

"I'll be right out here," Danae says after checking the vacant bathroom. "And don't forget to wash your hands."

"Duh," Emit says, closing the door.

Danae admires the portraits. She pauses on a painting of three familiar faces. The details of Enyo and Pemphredo painted in profile with Deino's oval face centered between them are vivid. Their long, dark hair is painted in an intricate weave.

"She really resembles Avi," Danae says to herself.

"Who's Avi?" Emit says.

Danae jumps. "I didn't hear you come out!"

He holds up his hands. "Clean and dry." He points to the painting. "That one looks like Xena."

Danae nods. "Xena is a descendant of Pemphredo, and Avi is a friend of ours. She is a descendant of Deino."

Emit frowns. "What does descendant mean?"

Danae takes Emit's hand and walks him back to the dining hall. The center door on the adjacent wall opens. A book floats out and glides towards Danae.

Emit gasps. "Mom, that book is flying!"

Danae laughs. "There is an entire library full of flying books through that door." She catches the volume hovering near her chest. "This book is your family tree."

The book opens to an illustration.

Danae points to the top. "Mui is one of your ancestors."

Emit looks up with his eyes crossed.

Danae laughs. "He is your many times great grandfather. That means you and Ora are descendants of Mui." She points to Itra's name and their names below.

"Cool," Emit whispers. He traces the line to Danae's name up to Hermes and stops. "We are descendants of Hermes, too?"

"Not exactly," Danae says, as she turns the page. "Leon and I are descendants of Zeus and Danae. And Hermes's father is Zeus, but his mother is Maia."

Emit scans the tree and his finger lands on Perseus. "He's family too?"

Danae nods. "A very distant relative."

The light stone hovering over Perseus's head dims and brightens as he paces the narrow corridor. He takes ten steps away from the rock blocking his exit—when he turns around, the rock is still directly behind him.

"This is an infinite loop from hell!" He punches the rock. He immediately regrets it and examines his bloody knuckles. "It's like the bridge to nowhere." He goes completely still, and his pulse kicks into overtime, causing his vision to blur. He reaches out and rests his hand against the wall.

"The ether," Perseus mumbles, sliding to the floor, "is what causes the infinite loop on the bridge to nowhere." He thumps his head against the wall. "This was not Ember's errand. This is her punishment for trespassing and throwing the hourglass into the ether abyss below the bridge." He closes his eyes and tries to slow his racing heart. "Andromeda!"

10

Elis finishes the play-by-play of their encounter with Perseus and Andromeda as he and Leon reach the square, glass tower.

"Elis!" Zana says, running and jumping into his arms.

Elis staggers back but holds on to Zana.

Leon nudges them forward away from the stairwell.

"Are you ok?" Anton asks, checking Elis over.

"I'm good, dad," Elis says, pushing Zana's curls out of his face. "Thanks to Leon and Danae."

Anton side hugs Leon. "Thank you."

Leon nods. "What's the status on Ora?"

"They identified a boulder outside of the revolutionary ember archway," Kaly says, looking at Anton. He nods. "And Ana is leading the group."

"Ana's awake?" Leon asks.

"You're squeezing me," Zana says, wiggling out of Elis's tight grasp.

"Ana is here?" Elis asks, going to the edge of the glass.

"You remember her?" Kaly asks.

"Of course." His breath fogs the glass, and he wipes it away with his sleeve. He searches the clearing below. "Was she here sleeping?"

Anton steps beside Elis and rests a hand on his shoulder. "Ana was in the future cavern a few days ago when it collapsed."

Elis turns to face Anton. "Is she hurt?"

"She's making a full recovery," Anton says, tipping his head to the clearing. "She was up talking and walking."

Elis nods and turns his focus back to the clearing.

"Do you know how they're managing the passage under the ember archways without the feathered cloaks?" Leon asks Kaly.

"Each of the kids and Hermes were given a cloak before they were taken," Kaly says. "Zana gave hers to Itra. Hermes came back just before they crossed."

"Elis, do you and Emit have cloaks on as well?" Leon asks.

"Yes, sorry I forgot about that detail," Elis says, turning his back to Leon and raising his arms out to the side.

A feathered cloak appears and hovers behind his lanky frame.

"Kaly," Leon says, turning around and extending his arms. The cloak turns and vanishes against Leon's back. "I'll get Emit's and take it to the others."

Zana hugs Leon around the waist. "She's the owl."

Leon looks down at Zana. "What do you mean?"

"The owl will dress in red," Zana says. "Her power will protect Ember's time."

"Her power controlled Elis and Hermes—she helped kidnap you and the twins."

"But Ember," Zana says.

Leon shakes his head. "Ember is not the boss! Especially when it comes to your safety."

"Be careful, please," Zana whispers.

Leon leans over and kisses the tip of her nose. "Always."

11

"The boulder is just around the bend," Ana says, wheezing.

Hermes pushes off.

"Rest here," Itra says, pointing to a tree stump.

She nods, trying to catch her breath.

Itra shades his eyes with his hand and looks up. He spots Hermes hovering behind a large tree.

Hermes points to the area Ana suggested and holds up two fingers.

Itra pushes off and slowly gains altitude until he spots Ora's brown curls. He feels a hand on his shoulder and teeters losing air.

"It's me!" Leon whispers.

"You nearly gave me a heart attack," Itra says. "The boys? Danae?"

"Safe at the castle," Leon says, nodding towards the rock. "Let's get her back."

Itra points to Hermes.

Leon raises his hand in the air and twirls two fingers.

Hermes nods and pulls back and up.

Itra and Leon spread out and fly high, spotting the woman pacing near the boulder.

"Hey!" Hermes shouts, flying over the tree straight towards Andromeda.

Andromeda lifts her jeweled hand and closes it into a tight fist, freezing Hermes. He hangs limp in the air.

"You fool!" Andromeda snarls. "Where is Perseus?"

Hermes grunts.

Andromeda releases her pinky finger from her fist, and Hermes coughs.

She glares at him. "Where is he?"

Leon hovers directly behind Andromeda and calls his staff. He winks at Ora and holds a finger over his mouth.

Ora nods and quietly stands up.

Hermes moves his jaw from side to side. "I wish I knew."

Itra lands next to Ora. She jumps up into his arms without making a sound. He points up and she nods.

"You're lying!" Andromeda bends her wrist and Hermes free falls towards the ground.

Leon double taps his staff and swings the translucent scythe—slicing through Andromeda's waist long braid. It falls to the ground, exposing her neck.

"Ah!" Andromeda screams. She releases her control over Hermes.

Hermes flips and redirects his flight path aiming feet first into Andromeda's back as she turns to face Leon.

"Did you think I came alone?" Hermes asks, shoving her an inch away from Leon's scythe.

Andromeda's coal rimmed eyes dart to the vacant boulder. She spits towards Leon.

"Now, now, little owl," Leon says. "You can play nice and live—or I can kill you and still sleep like a baby. Your choice."

Andromeda twists her hand.

Leon swings the scythe across her forearm slicing through the gold bangles. They fall a foot away from her heap of hair.

"Stop!" Andromeda says, baring her teeth. She huffs. "What do you want?"

"It's simple," Leon says. "Why?"

Andromeda frowns. "Why did you cut my hair? Great question."

Leon swings the scythe again and buzzes another inch off her ebony locks.

Her mouth falls open.

Hermes giggles.

"Answer carefully or die," Leon says.

Andromeda closes her mouth and audibly swallows. "Perseus."

"Perseus was banned from the Castle of Teskom seven years ago," Hermes says.

"He received a message from Ember," Andromeda says. She turns to Hermes. "You saw the envelope."

"That envelope was addressed to me," Hermes says, wiping the sweat off his brow. The afternoon sun glares down on them. "Not Perseus and his wanna be witch—I mean wife."

"Impossible."

"How did you know the passage that was given to my daughter?" Leon asks.

"Perseus's message from Ember," Andromeda says, "had the versus written out and instructions on when to arrive. I was to dress in red, like the message said." She looks down at her red tunic and cloak. "We were instructed to bring time and the compass to the past ember archway."

"And then what?" Leon asks.

Andromeda shrugs. "Perseus said he would know where and when after we completed the first task."

Hermes laughs. "And you believed him?"

She flicks her finger and Hermes flies back about ten feet. He lands on his back.

"That's enough." Leon taps his scythe to the ember glow and lowers the fiery tip to the ground.

A ring of fire surrounds her in an instant.

"You good?" Leon asks, nodding to Hermes.

Hermes brushes off the dirt and stands. "I may not sit right for a week." He winces as he takes a step.

"Make it stop!" Andromeda shrieks as the flames creep closer.

"Hermes, what do you think?" Leon asks. "Does she deserve any mercy?"

"Unlikely, but Zeus and Princess Danae may find her absence concerning."

"I'll tell you everything I know about the hourglass," Andromeda says, stomping out the flames closing in around her feet.

"Remove every piece of jewelry and toss them into the flames," Leon says.

"What? No!"

Leon lowers the staff towards the ground and the flames dance higher. "Hermes, have you ever had a smore?"

"Fine, fine!" Andromeda shouts. She holds her hand up and removes each ring. She struggles with her pinky ring twisting and pulling until it pops off and into the flames. She drops the others into the fire. She holds up her hands, which are now free of any gold or jewelry.

Leon releases the staff, and the flames drop.

Andromeda immediately bends to search the ground for her rings. "They're gone?"

"The fire was pretty hot." Hermes points and laughs at Andromeda's smoke-smudged face and new haircut. "Unlike you now."

Andromeda flicks her fingers once, then tries a second time. She stomps her foot. "Powerless." She stares at her hands.

"Start talking," Leon says. "Or the burning ring of fire will take more than your power."

She glares at Leon. "Have you no dignity or class?"

Leon smiles. "Nah, chucked that out the window after my last tour."

"Tour," Hermes says, "like a band?"

"Like war."

Andromeda straightens her posture and adjusts her bunched tunic. "The hourglass is in the ether abyss below the bridge to nowhere."

"Old news," Hermes says.

Andromeda glares at Hermes. "What do you mean old news?"

"We've known that for seven years," Leon says. "When did Perseus get the message from Ember to kidnap the kids?"

"Three days ago," Andromeda says.

Leon nods. "And the plan today?"

"Blown to bits," Andromeda says, turning to look towards the ember archway. "Is he dead?"

"Perseus?" Leon asks.

She nods and casts her eyes to the ground.

"He will be... when Danae finds him," Leon says.

Andromeda's head snaps up. "Princess Danae is here?"

Hermes laughs and winks at Leon. "We call her the queen."

Andromeda's face falls into a deep frown.

The sun dips below the tree line.

Leon surveys the area. "We need to get back inside."

"You have a history with rocks," Hermes teases, patting the boulder where Ora once sat.

She flares her nose and balls her fist. "What are you implying?"

"Turn around and put your hands behind your back," Leon says, stepping towards her.

She stomps her foot again. "Absolutely not!"

Leon calls his staff, shifting it from one hand to the other causing the ember glow to blur.

"I told you everything I know," Andromeda whines. "Let me go and I promise to never return."

Leon shakes his head and continues shifting the staff from side to side. "We still have more probing to do. But it will happen with fair judgement inside and in front of your peers."

"No." Andromeda takes a step back and bumps into a person. Hands reach down and pin her arms behind her back.

She bucks and twists to view the assailant. She has to tilt her head back so far that she nearly falls.

"Meet Junior," Leon says, releasing his staff and pulling a black plastic zip tie out of his cargo pocket.

Junior turns her so her back is towards Leon.

Leon loops the plastic around her wrists in a figure eight and threads the end through. He pulls until her wrists slide together.

"You just carry those around?" Hermes asks, coming to examine Andromeda's wrists.

"Yes, when you've worked security for as long as I have," Leon says, pointing to his watch. "I slide them in my pocket after putting on my watch every day."

"The others are waiting inside," Junior says, scanning the area. "Was she alone?"

"Minus Ora," Leon says, "yes."

Junior looks her over. "Nice haircut."

Andromeda spits at Junior's feet.

"Talk about class," Leon says, pushing her forward. "Walk."

She stumbles a few steps but walks towards the ember archway.

"I'll sweep the perimeter," Hermes says.

Leon nods. He shoves Andromeda forward again when she hesitates.

Junior follows with his back to Leon.

12

Hermes pushes off and flies along the tree line. He scans the woods for any movement before gaining altitude, then he spots a boat on the lake below.

Hermes drifts down over the vessel. A man on the top deck is standing with his arm raised. On closer inspection, he isn't blinking or moving outside of the rise and fall of the small wakes of the lake. *He's frozen in time.*

Hermes lands on the deck and waves a hand in front of the man's face. *He's breathing.* He turns to look where the man was staring and finds the dark outline of a cave on the face of the rocky hillside.

"My bet is that's Perseus's entry or exit point from the castle," Hermes says, patting the frozen man on the shoulder. "Thanks, man." He pushes off and flies towards the opening.

He lands and feels an instant drop in temperature. He adjusts his tunic and takes his light stone out of his pocket. Then he taps the stone and throws it forward.

The walls of the cave narrow to a large, wedged rock. As he nears the rock a crackle charge in the air raises every hair on his head. He backs away and looks for any additional entrances but pauses when he hears a grunt. *Wild boar?*

Then a voice speaks. "Andromeda, is that you?"

Hermes recognizes Perseus's voice immediately. "She's a little busy, but you can leave her a message."

"Hermes?" Perseus groans. "Did you kill her?"

"I'm not the criminal in the family." Hermes snickers. "But Danae might."

"Over Zeus's dead body," Perseus says.

"I never clarified which Danae," Hermes says, hearing a few footsteps shuffling closer.

"Stop with the games and get me out of here!"

"Are you stuck?" Hermes says, trying hard not to laugh.

"What do you think?" Perseus asks.

"Nah," Hermes says, stepping away from the rock. "I think you're doing just fine."

"You can't leave me here!" Perseus says, pounding on the rock.

"Oh, but I can and will." Hermes bows. "Sincerely, Flyboy." He pushes off and flies out of the cavern.

Hermes lands and steps under the ember archway. He spots Junior and Leon with Andromeda near the castle entrance. He flies over and lands beside Leon, just outside the castle door.

"All clear?" Leon asks.

"Almost," Hermes says. Andromeda twists to look at him. "Time is still frozen."

"Good to know," Leon says, handing Andromeda to Junior. "Take her to the dining hall. I want to see something before we begin our interrogation."

Junior squeezes Andromeda's arm. "Let's go," he says.

Andromeda jerks but Junior tightens his grip.

"Get your hands off me!"

Junior ignores her and marches forward forcing her to walk beside him. They follow the curved path through the conservatory towards the dining hall door.

Hermes waits until Junior and Andromeda are out of sight before he turns to Leon. "And I've located Perseus."

"Where?" Leon asks.

Hermes grins. "He's stuck in a cave behind a very large rock."

"Is he frozen, too?" Leon asks.

"Oh no, very much alive and pissed off."

Leon shakes his head and sighs. "We should have done more research on the time effects outside of the castle." He pulls out his light stone and taps it. "I want to check on the future cavern." He walks towards the stairwell leading down from the front entrance.

"Why?" Hermes asks, following Leon.

"To confirm what Teuta claimed happened," Leon says.

"Wait? What happened?"

Leon looks over his shoulder and raises an eyebrow. "About the collapse."

Hermes shakes his head.

Leon nods. "Oh, you were with the kids when Teuta broke the news." Leon starts his descent, picking up his pace down the spiral steps. "Teuta claims that the future cavern collapsed while Ana was down there."

"When?" Hermes asks, matching Leon's pace.

"Three days ago," Leon says.

"I thought I was the first one here," Hermes says. "I wasn't aware of anyone besides Teuta, and within a few hours, Junior and Xena arrived."

"Supposedly, Dita arrived a few hours after the collapse to aid in Ana's recovery."

"I thought Dita and Ana arrived after we were taken," Hermes says.

Leon pauses on the last step.

The tall wood and iron door is slightly ajar.

Leon calls his staff and uses the wooden end to slowly push the door open. The light hovering over his head floats into the dark space.

Hermes steps beside Leon. "It's like a bomb went off in the center." He points to the center of the cavern, a circle free from the rubble.

Leon picks through the various rocks with the end of his staff. Hermes flies up and checks the jagged stalagmites barely clinging to the ceiling.

"What was the phrase to activate the cavern wall?" Leon asks as Hermes lands.

"We are here, we are open, we are present."

Leon turns in a circle. "Our future window is officially busted."

"But we still have Ana," Hermes says, clamping a hand down on Leon's shoulder.

"Let's hope," Leon says. "We just need to get the hourglass back and the urtar stone balanced."

13

Leon and Hermes enter the dining hall to silence, although nearly every chair at the table is taken.

"Who died?" Hermes asks, taking in the somber faces.

Danae sniffles and turns to Leon and Hermes.

"It's Ana," Danae says, pushing her chair back from the table. "She collapsed when Itra brought her back through the ember archway."

"Dita tried to help," Anton says, reaching a hand over to Dita. Her head is buried in her arms resting on the table. "I saw her lean over Ana just before she disappeared."

Dita raises her head up and wipes away the stream of tears. "I scanned her before she woke." She shakes her head. "She was weak, but otherwise recovered. I don't understand why she collapsed." She looks at Leon. "She was ice cold. I didn't get a pulse before she vanished into thin air."

"We immediately searched the castle," Danae says. "But Teuta claims she isn't here. And I can't feel her presence here either."

"Where is Teuta?" Leon asks, looking around the room.

"Checking if Ana was returned home," Itra says, holding Ora.

"I might have an explanation," Xena says, looking up from a book.

"Something to do with time?" Leon asks.

Xena nods.

"Hermes found a man on a boat," Leon says, "He was motionless but still breathing."

"Frozen in time," Itra whispers.

Hermes nods.

Leon points to Itra, Ora, Hermes, and Junior. "The five of us were wearing a cloak when we crossed the ember archway to the revolutionary dimension. But Ana wasn't because she's from there."

"Andromeda survived just fine," Hermes argues.

Junior shakes his head and points to the occupied chair facing the corner of the room. "A cloak flew off her the second we entered the dining hall."

"Why is she sitting in the corner?" Hermes asks.

"She kept spitting on Junior," Danae says. "She is a vile woman."

"Says the imposter!" Andromeda yells from the corner.

Leon laughs. "She figured out you aren't 'that' Danae."

Danae nods.

"We need to get her out of here," Leon says. "Do we have a secure holding cell?"

The door parallel to the portrait hallway swings open.

"Do you know where that goes?" Leon asks, gesturing to the open door.

"The Kelmend war room and suites," Hermes says.

The chair holding Andromeda zips across the hall.

"Ah!" Andromeda screams.

The chair clears the doorway, and the door slams shut.

The echo of her scream fades.

"Let's hope that was a temporary solution," Hermes says. He chuckles. "Pretty sure Perseus will be pissed off if we just killed his new wife."

"He's alive?" Danae asks.

"Wedged behind a rock inside a cave in the revolutionary dimension," Hermes says, pointing down.

"And you left him there?" Itra asks. "What if he escapes? Or worse, what if he comes back for the kids?"

"I believe Ember is punishing him," Hermes says. "The passages of time used to access the hedge maze inside the castle have an energy that crackles."

Xena nods, recalling her trip with Enyo and Noel to recover a missing shield. "I remember that feeling. An almost static charge to the air when I crossed the threshold."

Hermes nods. "I felt that same sensation near the rock. I believe he's stuck there for as long as Ember deems necessary."

"That's somewhat comforting," Danae says, "but I would still like an answer on how they were granted entry to the Castle of Teskom."

"I'll keep watch over him until we find a more permanent solution," Junior says, nodding to Dita. "Can you stay in the present cavern?"

Dita nods. "Of course."

"Hermes, can you open a doorway to the cavern after I put a cloak back on?" Junior asks.

A cloak flies into the room.

The kids gasp and point.

Junior stands and extends his arms. The cloak drifts and drapes over him before vanishing into his tunic.

Hermes taps the gold ring on his left thumb. "Right." He stands next to Junior. "Protect time, unite to fight. Ember of mine." A door opens to the boulder blocking Perseus's exit.

Junior nods to Dita. "If anything changes, let them know." He walks through the new door.

"I'll be watching but keep me in the loop," Dita says, tapping her temple. She stands and walks towards the conservatory door.

14

"Let's try to tackle the next problem—time," Leon says, walking over to Itra and Ora. He kneels level with Ora. "Ora, can you tell me what happened when she took you under the ember archway?"

Ora sits up and pulls away from Itra. "My shoulder burned." She twists to show Leon the back of her right shoulder.

Itra pulls back Ora's shirt. Her birthmark with the circle of twelve red dots appears intact but with one slight change.

"Danae!" Itra exclaims.

Danae rushes to Ora. "What's wrong?"

"The dot that was darker than the others... it's moved," Itra says, pointing. "Her darkest mark was the sixth from the top."

"And now the seventh," Danae says.

The library door opens and a book flies towards the table. Xena catches a thick, royal blue, book with an hourglass embossed on the cover. It falls open, and she turns it towards the others. She taps the page with her finger.

"That's like mine," Emit says, pointing to the illustration on the page. "I have that mark here." He twists pointing to the back of his left shoulder.

Danae rounds the table to Emit. She pulls back Emit's shirt and inspects his left shoulder. She silently counts twelve red dots and ensures the top one is still the darkest. "You're good." She pats his cheek. "It's still the same."

"What does the caption say?" Kaly says, turning back to the page and squinting at the small text.

Xena turns the book back towards herself. "Time will begin and start again when they align with the divine."

"Another riddle?" Leon asks, standing.

Xena waves him over. Leon looks over her shoulder. She flips back a page and points to a passage written in loopy blue ink.

"The hour to all will fall when time crosses the line," Leon reads. "A compass can guide time inside to begin again or tip the end. He must decide."

"Elis," Danae says, "did you try to guide Emit when you crossed under the ember archway?"

Elis shrugs. "I tried to keep Emit away from those lunatics. Does that count?"

"Does this explain why time wasn't frozen when we crossed through to save them without cloaks?" Leon asks.

"Possibly," Kaly says. "Either that or they can't stop time in the past."

Teuta appears next to Hermes.

Hermes leaps away. "Not cool!"

Teuta jingles the bell around her neck and plasters a wide grin across her face. "Mystery solved."

"What do you mean?" Anton asks, standing so fast the chair teeters.

Elis catches it and pulls it away from his father.

"Is Ana alive?" Anton continues.

Teuta nods. "She's alive but frozen along with everyone else in her home dimension." She skips around the table. "And I checked the other dimensions too. Time is frozen everywhere but here and the past."

Ora climbs down from Itra's lap and marches towards Teuta. "You are Ember's mark maker."

Danae and Itra glance at each other. They shrug and frown.

"Ah, why yes I am." Teuta bends closer to Ora.

"Ember said you would teach us about our gifts," Ora says.

"When did you speak to Ember?" Itra asks, looking from Emit to Danae. They shake their heads.

"I've always spoken to Ember," Ora says, turning towards the table. Every face looks back at her with mouths slightly ajar except for Elis. He winks at Ora. "Elis and I have always heard her whispers."

"The dreams?" Anton asks, turning towards Elis. "You knew it was Ember this entire time?"

"Not exactly," Elis says. "Ora and I have had similar dreams, and we've heard the same phrases. But I never knew it was Ember until Zana read the message to us last night."

Zana holds up her hand. "I know how to align time."

Everybody turns their attention to Zana.

Zana points to Ora. "Ora is the beginning." She points to Emit. "Emit is the end." She points to Elis. "Elis is the compass to guide time." She points to herself. "I am the divine." She smiles and looks around. The wide-eyed stare from every adult in the room makes her roll her eyes. "Mama, you've always called me 'my little divine'."

Kaly nods and smiles. "You are my little divine and according to your lineage, you're a divine of Ember. She is your ancestor."

Teuta pats Ora on the head. "It looks like my lessons are complete."

Ora frowns. "What lessons?"

"As Zana stated," Teuta says, "each of you controls an aspect of time, but it is the four of you together that completes the infinite loop."

The dining hall falls dark. A bright line of light appears and twirls creating an elongated figure eight.

"Time is infinite," Teuta says, "but it can be slowed by force."

The figure eight unravels to a straight line of light.

Teuta points to one end. "Elis, focus on reconfiguring the line into the infinity symbol."

Elis stands. "How?"

Teuta steps closer to the line so the light illuminates her face. She taps on her temple. "Do you recall the phrase you used to slow time with Danae against the rogue descendants?"

Elis glances at Danae.

She nods.

Elis says, "Time will bend. Ember will descend."

"Great," Teuta says. "Now focus on the phrase as you try to move the line."

Elis nods and focuses on the middle of the line. *Time will bend. Ember will descend.* He thinks the phrase several times, but the line remains flat.

He turns to Teuta. "It's not working," he says.

"Because you need time," Teuta says. "Ora and Emit, please stand beside Elis."

Emit and Ora stand on either side of Elis.

"Try again," Teuta says.

Elis frowns. "And do what?"

"Guide time," Teuta says.

Elis looks at Emit. "Take that end." He points to the end on the left. "And Ora, please take the other end."

Ora nods and raises her hand.

Emit follows her lead and raises his hand.

"Time will bend," Elis says. "Ember will descend."

The ends waver up and down.

Zana stands and walks towards the three of them. She extends her hands and slowly brings them above her head.

The ends of the line match her movements.

Zana laces her fingers together over her head, and the line of light merges.

"Wow," Hermes murmurs.

"That's great!" Teuta says, rocking up on her toes. "Elis twist the circle to create a figure eight."

Elis lifts his hands, moving one towards his chest and pushing the other out and down. *Like riding a bike, peddle.* He repeats the motion and peddles clockwise.

The circle bends. The shape folds into a figure eight.

The kids let their hands fall to their sides and their eyes remain glued to the infinity loop.

Hermes claps breaking the silent revery.

Teuta flutters around the kids. "You did it!"

The infinity loop fades as a light stone illuminates the dining hall.

Ora looks up at Elis. "Do you remember doing this in a dream?"

Elis nods. "I do."

"Do you remember what happens next?" Ora asks, pointing at the door to the conservatory.

The group turns to see what she is pointing at. The door swings open.

Two cloaked figures walk in, and Leon calls his staff.

15

One figure drops their hood and smiles. "Are we late?"

"Enyo!" Xena and Kaly say in unison.

Enyo smiles. "May I reintroduce Deino?"

Deino removes her hood and dips her head toward the onlookers.

"How did you get in?" Leon asks. "Teuta claimed time was frozen in all dimensions.

Teuta clears her throat. "Not exactly. The past was not frozen."

"Avi called for our help," Enyo says. "Otherwise, we would have been here sooner."

"Who's Avi?" Zana asks, poking Kaly's side.

"A friend and the woman who brought you to us," Kaly says, pushing a hair behind Zana's ear.

"Is Avi ok?" Xena asks.

"When we arrived," Deino says, following her sister to the table, "she, um... was disabled. But we communicated with her." She taps her temple. "She was on her way here when time slowed to a stop. What has happened?"

Hermes spends the next twenty minutes going over the future cavern collapse, the kidnapping attempt by Perseus, and the capture of Andromeda.

"Andromeda is here?" Enyo asks, looking around.

"Where is she?" Deino asks.

Leon gestures to the closed door across the room. "Secured to a chair in there."

"And did she explain how they managed to breech the castle?" Enyo asks.

"We haven't interrogated her yet," Leon says, looking at Teuta. "Can you bring her back into the dining hall?"

"Me?" Teuta asks, pointing to her chest. Leon nods. Her eyes widen. She shakes her head.

Leon frowns. "What is it?"

Danae holds up a hand. "I can't feel Andromeda's presence here anymore."

"Did you let her escape?" Itra asks, pointing a finger at Teuta.

Teuta holds up both hands and takes two steps back. "I haven't."

"But you know something," Leon says.

Teuta nods. "I can show you, but..." She looks at the wide eyes of the three youngest children staring at her. "I'm not sure if it is child friendly."

Danae and Itra share a quick glance and then focus on Kaly and Leon.

Kaly stands. "I'll show them the library."

"I want to stay," Emit whines.

"Go with Kaly," Itra says. "Kaly can still hear what's going on in here, right?" He turns to Teuta.

Teuta nods.

Ora and Zana follow Kaly without a word. Emit trudges behind them, arms folded and bottom lip protruding.

Once the library door closes, the dining hall dims. A three-dimensional bird's-eye image of Andromeda falling, still tied to the chair, appears above the table.

Andromeda bounces when the legs of the chair slam into the ground.

"Help!" Her own voice echoes back. She tilts her head to look for a door, but only finds darkness. She blinks a few times, and her eyes adjust. She can barely see the outline of her legs.

She attempts to stand. One ankle is still secured to the chair, but the other has come loose. She reaches her free foot out and pats around. *Dirt?*

Andromeda sighs. "Can anyone hear me?"

"Shh."

"Who's there?" Andromeda twists around. The chair wobbles back. She leans forward to balance it.

"You've trespassed and taken something that doesn't belong to you."

A woman? Andromeda sneers. "Face me and speak those accusations." She pulls against the restraints, but the zip ties cut into her wrists.

"You're rather confident you could survive that encounter."

Andromeda's skin prickles, and she slows her movements. "You're threatening me?"

"It's no threat but justice."

"How dare you?" Andromeda says, scanning the room. "Ember sent Perseus a message to arrive at a specific time and do what we did."

A breath of air tickles Andromeda's exposed neck. She jerks her head back. "Face me, you coward!"

"I am."

Andromeda strains her eyes. "I see nothing."

"You see what you want."

Andromeda blinks twice and gasps. She glares at the reflection of her own face staring back at her from a shimmering surface. "What kind of crap is this?"

"Your vanity consumes you."

Andromeda turns her head from side to side. Her ebony hair is unevenly cut to her chin. *My hair! I will kill that bastard!*

"Leon is quite the barber."

"What happened to her hair?" Deino asks, leaning forward.

The streaming feed pauses.

"And I don't see any jewelry?" Enyo points to Andromeda's image.

"She lost her jewelry and her hair during our rescue of Ora," Leon says, studying the image of Andromeda's hands.

The footage continues to play.

"Shut up!" Andromeda kicks out her free leg and finds only air. "Get to the point!"

"Answer three questions honestly and I will release you."

"Fine," Andromeda says, biting the inside of her lip. "Ask away. I have nothing to hide."

"Where did Perseus find the message to return to the Castle of Teskom?"

Andromeda huffs. "It was on the table when we returned to our room three, no, four days ago."

The restraint on her left wrist pops. She rolls her shoulder, shakes out her hand, and flexes her wrist. She reaches up and touches her shorn hair.

"What did the message say exactly?"

Andromeda taps her lips. "Arrive through the cave in three days. Find the cloaks to fly and bind a line with time, the

74

compass, and the divine. Before the day is one, Ember's compass will guide time inside to dial the light and retrieve the stone before night. The owl will dress in red. Her power will protect Ember's time."

"And?"

"That's it," Andromeda says, tugging her bound wrist and ankle.

"Tsk, tsk."

"I read the card," Andromeda says. "That's what it said."

Andromeda's reflection fades and the room fills with white light. She shades her eyes with her free hand and blinks until her eyes adjust again. She notices the dirt floor appears to be ash and the stone walls are smudged in black peaks.

"What is this place?" Andromeda demands.

"It's where liars burn."

Andromeda twists her neck to both sides. *No exits?*

"Last question."

The putrid smell of burnt hair wafts across Andromeda's face. She grimaces and holds her breath.

"Did the message invite you inside the Castle of Teskom?"

She inhales through her mouth. "No."

The final zip tie around her ankle snaps. She stands and moves the chair around. She rolls her shoulder forward. She pulls and assesses her tethered wrist.

"That answer is all I needed to hear."

The zip tie falls from Andromeda's wrist. She looks around the space again and the smell of burning hair intensifies. She pinches her nose. "Keep your end of the deal." She walks towards the wall. She inspects the stones for any gaps or seams. "Let me go."

The room falls to darkness once again.

Andromeda shrills out a string of incoherent curses.

"You could've been completely free." The last word echoes back in a distant, mocking whisper. *"Free, free, free."*

Andromeda stomps her foot and pounds her fist against the stones. "Let me out!"

"Two honest answers and one lie will light a fire."

The floor glows with specks of red.

"Wait stop!"

A ring of fire ignites and pushes her away from the wall. She stubs her toes on the chair and hops on one foot. The flames dance further inside igniting another circle.

"Pause it!" Anton says.

The image freezes.

"Elis, please go join Kaly," Anton says.

"But dad," Elis protests.

"Son, I do not allow you to watch R-rated horror movies at home, right?"

Elis nods.

"Well, I will not allow you to watch any more of this madness on the same principle." Anton points towards the library door. "Go, now."

Elis slides his chair back and stomps over to the library. He pushes open the door and slams it behind him.

"Pardon my teenager's attitude," Anton says.

Danae pats his arm. "He's a good kid."

Teuta waves her hand, and the streaming continues.

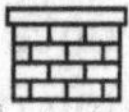

"Please stop," Andromeda says. She coughs and covers her mouth with her tunic. She kneels on the floor and curls into a

76

ball. "Please." She wipes away the tears. "I've told you everything I know."

"You left out one fine detail."

Andromeda coughs again. "What?"

"The envelope."

Andromeda shakes her head. "You only asked what the message said."

"Whose name was on the envelope?"

"I never saw the envelope," Andromeda says, squeezing her eyes closed. "Perseus opened it and passed me the card."

The fire crackles and pops. The heat is upon her. Sweat dampens her tunic and hair.

"Ah, but you saw the envelope."

Andromeda curls in tighter. "No!"

"He showed it to Hermes in the war room."

"That was a different message," Andromeda says.

"And where did that message come from?"

"Please, I can't breathe," Andromeda says, her voice hoarse from coughing.

"Answer me."

"Perseus said it was in the pocket of his tunic this morning." Andromeda tries to sit up, but the smoke is too thick making it hard to catch her breath. She coughs. "Are you—coughs again—implying the original message was for Hermes?"

Hermes pounds a fist on the table.

The frame pauses on Andromeda's furrowed brow.

"Perseus showed me an envelope from Ember," Hermes says.

"How did you know to arrive here?" Leon asks, facing Hermes.

Teuta holds up her hand. "I came and got him upon Ember's request."

"Ember knew your message was taken?" Danae asks.

Hermes shrugs. "I guess."

The footage continues.

Clap, clap, clap

Andromeda glares into the smoke as the clapping continues to echo all around her. "Show yourself!" she says.

"Smoke-filled chambers are good for two things."

"Oh, is that so?" Andromeda says, coughing into her sleeve.

"Meat and discovering the truth of a useless toy bride."

"How dare you!" Andromeda spits.

"Tani!"

"I really hate that word," Leon mumbles.

"What word?" Hermes asks.

"T-a-n-i," Leon says.

Teuta giggles and dances to Leon's side. "Oh, but you loved saying it when you were the messenger."

"Only because it was necessary to send you and that traitor Athena away." Leon turns to Hermes. "Your family has quite the reputation to live up to."

"I aim to squash the shame they've brought to our lines," Hermes says and winks. "Starting with Perseus."

16

"Kaly, can we please go back out there?" Emit asks, pointing to the door. "They're done with the movie!"

"Emit!" Kaly says. "Were you watching through the keyhole?"

Ora giggles.

"You were distracting me?" Kaly asks, pointing to Ora.

"Maybe," Ora says.

"You two are double the trouble!" Kaly yanks open the door. "Danae, do they always tag team?"

Itra and Danae laugh and nod.

Emit skips out smiling.

Danae reigns in her laughter. "Emit, what did you do?"

He slides to a stop, raising both hands. "It wasn't me."

Ora and Zana stop behind Emit and are hiding behind their hands, whispering.

"Ok, you two," Danae says. "I think you may owe Aunt Kaly an apology."

"But mom," Emit whines.

"Don't but mom," Itra says.

Emit huffs and turns to Kaly. "I'm sorry I asked Ora to distract you."

Danae coughs and eyes Ora.

Ora drops her hand and turns to Kaly. "Me too, I'm sorry."

Elis exits the library with a stack of books. "I think I may have solved one of our problems."

"What did you find?" Xena asks, taking a few of the books off the top.

"I need to find the hourglass before Chronos," Elis says.

A book flies out from the middle of the stack. It opens and plops onto the table. Everyone leans over the book and gasps.

"She kept her word," Danae whispers.

Emit pushes on Danae's hip. "What is it? I can't see."

Danae scoots to the side.

"Who kept their word, mama?" Ora asks.

"A princess," Danae says.

"A real princess?" Zana asks.

Danae nods. "Her father was a king, and she married a man named Zeus."

Emit turns around and catches a book with a tree on the cover.

"What do you have there?" Itra asks, leaning over Emit's shoulder.

"I saw Zeus's name in the tree thing mom showed me earlier," Emit says, tracing his finger over the family tree. "Here! Zeus and Maia. And Danae?" Emit frowns. "Mom, you married Zeus too?"

Hermes laughs.

80

Emit turns to Hermes. "Your name is on here too."

Hermes nods. "Of course. And you are a descendant of Zeus and Princess Danae." He points to Danae. "And your mom, Danae, but also a different woman." He murmurs. "With a jerk son."

"Is that true?" Ora asks, tugging Danae's arm.

"It is," Danae says. "And she did us a huge favor seven years ago and hid the hourglass Perseus stole from the vault below." She points to the floor. "And Ember showed the family a message. A teenage Elis would find the hourglass below a sundial in the courtyard inside the City of Time."

"But Chronos knows where the hourglass is," Itra says.

Danae frowns. "How do you know that?"

"Ana," Itra says. "When we were walking to the ember archway, she explained what she saw in the future cavern and the dreams she had been having the week before arriving."

"And?" Leon asks.

"Chronos is near, watching our every move," Itra says, rolling his shoulders forward and sighing. "Her vision showed him waiting in the shadows and following the children to the courtyard. He takes Ora to bribe Elis to exchange her for the hourglass."

Deino points to Xena. "We need Pem."

Xena nods. "I'll head to the present cavern now."

"Wait," Kaly says. "What are you suggesting?"

Deino and Enyo exchange a glance.

Enyo nods to Xena.

Xena places a hand on Kaly's shoulder. "Pem can transform into Ora and bait Chronos."

"And if we can get Avi here," Deino says, "she can keep Pem from any real harm."

Zana holds up her hand. "What do you mean transform?"

Xena kneels next to Zana. "You know the mirror necklace Aunt Pem wears?"

Zana nods.

"It gives her the ability to use magic."

Zana's pupils double.

"She can change her appearance to match any woman she meets," Xena says.

Zana nods. "Right, and I'm the tooth fairy."

"Ha!" Leon barks a laugh.

The other adults snicker and laugh as well.

Xena stands and shakes her head. "I see your sense of humor has rubbed off swimmingly, Leon."

Leon raises his hands. "And what makes you think your niece isn't to blame."

Kaly laughs and Zana rolls her eyes.

"Laughter aside," Enyo says. "We still need to fix time."

Laughter ceases immediately.

"Way to kill the vibe, Enyo," Hermes mutters.

Enyo cuts him a look. "We are facing Chronos, and we need every advantage possible."

17

Andromeda drops with a thud. A cloud of dirt surrounds her.

"Ugh," Andromeda groans. She winces as she gets to her hands and knees. She sits back on her heels and blinks until her eyes adjust to the darkness.

"Perseus," Andromeda whispers to herself.

A sliver of flickering light emerges.

She sucks in a breath.

A shadow blocks the new light source.

"He's not with you?" a man asks.

Andromeda examines the figure walking towards her. She scrambles to her feet and takes a few steps back as the man towers nearly a foot in height over her.

"Who are you?" Andromeda stammers.

"Where is time?"

Andromeda cowers.

"Where are they!" His volume rattles the dirt.

"Inside the castle," Andromeda mutters.

"You failed." The man lowers his face nose to nose with Andromeda.

The white whiskers of his beard tickle her face.

"And your useless husband?" he asks.

Andromeda leans her head back and examines the face in front of her. "We were separated, and I was captured."

"You were bested by time?"

Andromeda frowns. "Bested? It was three against one, counting Ember's pet with the scythe, the giant, and the freaking fly boy, Hermes."

"Hmm," the man grunts.

She glares at his smirk. "Who are you?"

He steps back and strokes his beard.

"Well?" Andromeda says, folding her arms across her chest.

"Father Time," he says, "is one of my many titles."

Andromeda drops her hands to her sides and straightens her spine to her full height. "Liar."

He chuckles. "You dare to call me a liar?"

"Chronos isn't real!" Andromeda says. "Just a damn fairy tale." She sneers at the old man.

"I can see why your father left you tied to a rock to drown with the tide."

"How dare you!" Andromeda shoves the man in the chest, but her hands only find air. "What the..." She tries to throw a quick jab towards the man's throat, but her fist never lands.

"You insolent child."

Andromeda bolts around the man, but her motion slows before she can reach the door. She is yanked back to her starting position in front of his sneer.

"I did not say you could leave."

Andromeda tries to run again. She grunts a muffled, "Help!" but she can't move her mouth or a single muscle. *I can't even blink!*

He turns his back and walks towards the door. "Think on your bad behavior while I track down your worthless husband."

No, no, no!

18

"Do any of those books say how to fix time?" Leon asks, scanning the books on the long dining table.

Elis holds up a blue book with a compass on the cover. "I think so, but most of the pages are blank." He places the book on the table. "How do you make the words appear?"

"Hapur," Danae and Kaly say in unison.

The book opens and the pages flip to the back before it closes again.

Elis thumbs through the book, but the pages are still blank.

"Maybe only you can give it permission," Itra says.

Elis nods and places his palm on the cover. "Hapur."

The book shakes and lifts from the table.

Elis yanks his hand back.

The light stone overhead dims as the book opens.

Twelve red dots appear in a circle around the perimeter of the dome over the table. Each dot lights up once and dims except two.

"Twelve and seven," Itra says, pointing up.

"Teuta," Danae says. "Can you explain how this helps us restart time?"

Teuta prances up to Elis. "Guide Ora back to balance the time."

Ora comes to Elis's side. He extends his hand to her. She takes his hand and nods.

"How?" Elis asks, turning back to Teuta.

"Like before," Teuta says, "use the same phrase."

Ora squeezes Elis's hand and raises her free hand palm up towards the dome.

"Time will bend," Elis says. "Ember will descend."

Ora twists her wrist counterclockwise.

The light at the seventh mark flickers.

Zana walks to Ora's side. She leans over and whispers, "Think six."

The light flips to the sixth mark, aligning with the top.

Ora winces and twists around to look at her shoulder blade.

Danae pulls back her top. "It's back at the original mark. Does it hurt?"

"It just stung a little this time," Ora says, hugging Danae.

Teuta claps. "Great job! I'll check in with Ana first and then fetch Avi." She twirls and vanishes.

Danae strokes Ora's hair and looks over at Itra. "No one said anything about pain!"

Itra's nostrils flare. "I know," he says.

"It's ok daddy," Ora says, hugging him around the waist.

Itra leans over and picks her up. He snuggles Ora's neck. "I love you."

"I love you, too," Ora says, patting Itra's cheek.

Xena clears her throat. "I'll go get Pem."

"And I'll do a perimeter sweep," Hermes says.

Kaly looks up at the dome. The sky is streaked with lines of pink. "It's late. How about we get some dinner and show the kids their suites?"

Anton shakes his head. "We should go home." He puts a hand on Elis's shoulder.

Enyo glances over at her sister. "I'm sorry, but we still need him here."

Anton turns to face Enyo. "Look I know Elis has a role to play." He squeezes Elis's shoulder. "But it's not safe. We saw that this morning. Ember is not protecting them." He glances at Ora. "And causing them pain. We're done."

Deino shakes her head. "The hourglass with the urtar stone is recovered by Elis and Elis only."

Zana raises her hand. "What is an urtar stone?"

Kaly turns to Zana. "The urtar stone is better known as the stone of judgement."

Zana scrunches her nose.

"Think of it like a balance of good and bad," Kaly says, holding her hands palm up and level. "Like an old scale." She drops one hand and raises the other and then brings them level again. "Do you understand?"

"Kind of," Zana says.

"Can we circle back?" Anton asks, pointing at Deino. "How do you know it has to be Elis?"

"Our sister Pemphredo," Deino says. "She has dreams, like Ana, of future events. She has seen Elis remove the hourglass before an earthquake breaks the stones around the sundial."

Teuta appears beside Anton with Avi.

Avi straightens her long cardigan. "I like using my ring to create a door instead of using the portal method." She rubs her stomach.

"You'll get used to it!" Leon and Danae say in unison.

"You two could be twins," Ora says, pointing to Avi and Deino.

Deino smiles. "Our genes are strong."

Avi nods and pulls her long, dark, wavy hair over her shoulder.

Teuta smirks. "I see we are all present except for Xena, Hermes, Junior, and Dita."

"Hermes is flying the perimeter," Itra says. "Xena is fetching Pem."

"Junior is babysitting Perseus in the cave," Danae says, "and Dita is monitoring him from the present cavern."

"What is a present cavern?" Emit asks.

"A magic cavern below," Danae says.

Emit frowns.

"It's like a video call," Danae says. "We can see and speak to another person blessed by Ember from within that cavern."

"Cool!" Emit squirms in his chair. "Can I try it?"

"Maybe later," Danae says, facing Teuta. "Where's Ana?"

"She's resting," Teuta says, avoiding eye contact with Danae.

"What do you mean?" Anton says.

"I couldn't wake her," Teuta says, "but she's breathing. I've left her in her home to give her for more time to recover."

Kaly places a hand on Anton's arm. "She's ok."

"You can't know that for sure!" Anton says, shaking her hand off.

"Dad," Elis says, teary.

Anton sighs and hugs Elis. "I'm sorry, son. It's been a long day."

"Can we have the next conversation with food?" Danae suggests. "I think we could all use a bit of refreshment or liquid support."

A plate appears on the table next to Emit and he uncovers a hot pizza. "I'm never leaving here!"

The aroma of cheese entices the others to follow Emit's lead. They sit around the table, and one by one, a covered dish appears in front of each person.

Ora uncovers her plate. "Look mom, mac cheese!"

"What is mac cheese?" Deino asks.

"Seriously?" Zana points to Ora's plate. "You've never had macaroni and cheese?"

Deino smiles. "Never. Is it good?"

"The best!" Ora says, holding up her fork full of yellow noodles with a string of cheese still attached to the dish. "Do you want to try it?"

Deino shakes her head. "I'll take your word for it."

"Where are you from?" Zana asks.

Deino glances at Kaly.

Kaly smiles. "It's your story," she says to Deino.

Deino nods. "Enyo and I are from your past."

Ora's face pales a bit. "Are you ghosts?"

Enyo smiles and shakes her head. "There is a past ember archway."

Elis raises his hand. "But to what dimension?"

"We are technically part of the castle's dimension. Before Ember split the world."

88

"What are dimensions?" Zana asks.

"There are five ember archways in the clearing," Itra says, pointing towards the conservatory. "Like the ones Emit, Ora, and Elis were taken through."

Zana nods.

"One goes to the past, one to the future, and three archways go to parallel dimensions." He holds up his hands with his palms facing each other. He closes one fist. "Ana is from the revolutionary dimension. It's similar to our world, but there are no wars, only peace and prosperity." He closes his other fist. "Our world is called the communist dimension for obvious reasons, as you've learned about our history in school. And the third is the Ottoman dimension, where the Ottoman empire still rules the world."

"Why did the worlds split into three?" Elis asks.

"Ember," Teuta says. "She did it to protect the knowledge stored here and to establish a balance of power between dimensions."

"A power balance is required after Chronos is banished to the helix prison," Deino says.

"You mean was banished," Kaly says. Then she hesitates. "Right?"

Deino shakes her head. "When Chronos created his new form through Pax, he created a time loop in the past. The seven days before Ember's banishment have been repeating for the last seven years."

"He can do that?" Anton asks.

"He is space and time," Enyo says.

"Why are we just hearing of this now?" Danae asks.

"We didn't discover the loop until after we were all tossed out of the castle seven years ago," Enyo says, scowling at Teuta.

Teuta rolls her eyes. "I am just the messenger."

"We've had contact with Hermes over the years," Danae says. "Why didn't he say anything?"

"Because it's not common knowledge," Deino says. "When the loop resets, it wipes any memory of the previous week, making the events of the week like new for each person. But those with the gift of sight saw through the mirage."

"And you didn't think we should know this?" Xena asks.

"As long as the loop reset," Enyo says, looking at the twins, "we knew time was safe and Chronos was unable to break the events leading to his demise."

"Seven years," Xena whispers, shaking her head.

"It doesn't add up," Leon says. "Hermes has aged. He's not the same teenage boy that appeared in the hedge maze seven years ago." He points to Enyo. "How do you explain that?"

"The events of the seven days are the same," Deino says, "but we still evolved. That's why the loop remains undetected by the masses."

Enyo nods. "It took us four months to confirm our theory about the number of days and when the reset happens."

"And who else knows about this?" Kaly asks.

"As far as we know," Enyo says, "only Princess Danae."

"And the hourglass?" Teuta asks. "Did Princess Danae keep her word?"

"I did," Princess Danae says from the door to the conservatory. "Pardon my tardiness. Am I interrupting?" She bows her head towards the wide-eyed stares piercing her from the table.

"She looks like you, mama!" Ora says, pointing.

"I've noticed," Itra mutters.

"I don't believe we have been properly introduced," Princess Danae says, offering her hand to Itra.

Itra takes and shakes her hand.

"Your purple dress is really pretty," Zana says.

Princess Danae kneels to her level. "And you are?"

Kaly stands and steps between the princess and Zana. "My daughter."

19

"Let me out!" Perseus yells hoarsely.

Junior laughs.

"At the very least," Perseus says, wrapping a hand around his throat, "spare me something to drink!"

Junior walks away from the large rock blocking Perseus's exit and stops near the ledge overlooking Lake Shkoder. "I wish I could—but the lake is, um, a hundred meters down or more, and I am fresh out of cups."

Perseus groans.

Junior lifts his gaze to the shadowed peaks of the Montenegro mountains.

The last bit of sunlight disappears, and the clouds cover any sign of the moon.

Junior releases the clasps at his shoulders and his tunic sleeves unravel. He rubs his hands together.

"Are they going to kill her?" Perseus whispers.

"Are who going to kill her?" Junior asks.

"Leon and Hermes," Perseus says.

"I would if you stole my children," Junior says.

"Do you even have kids?"

Junior smiles. "That is none of your business."

"Ah," Perseus says. "Do you know how long Ember will keep me down here?"

Junior chuckles. "Get comfortable."

A scuffle of rocks hits the cavern walls.

"Kicking rocks," Junior says. "How mature."

"Junior," Dita says.

Junior whirls around, but the cavern is dark. *"Where are you?"*

"Still in the present cavern," Dita says.

Junior jumps out of the cavern. His cloak pushes him up and he hovers out over the middle of the lake.

"Alright, what's up?"

"Brother," Dita scolds, *"you probably shouldn't be hanging out, hovering above the lake."*

"It's dark enough," Junior says. *"No one can see me. What's on fire now?"*

"Princess Danae just arrived."

"Shit," Junior says. *"Do we know why?"*

"Apparently Chronos managed to put a time loop in the past dimension set for seven days before Ember throws him in the helix."

"But how?"

"Enyo claims he set it before Pax and the urtar stone were shoved into the hourglass."

"And it held after Pax was captured?"

"Yes. Princess Danae and the sisters kept this secret even from Hermes, for the last seven years."

Junior laughs. *"And I thought our family was great at keeping secrets."*

"Not a time for humor the loop is cracking," Dita says.

"What do you mean?"

"The loop normally resets at noon on the seventh day, but it's glitched twice in the last twenty-four hours. It went from day to night instantly. Night lasted for three hours and then flipped back to daytime."

Junior loses elevation for a moment and then corrects his position. *"Confusing, but why is that a concern?"*

"Right before dusk, the sun reset to high noon and an earthquake struck the center of a town near the sundial."

"The hourglass," Junior says.

"Gone."

"And who do they think has the damn thing now?" Junior asks, flying closer to the cavern's opening.

"Two men reported they saw a young man matching Elis's description wearing a black object around his wrist near the sundial moments before the earthquake."

"But Elis is sitting inside the castle and hasn't left since they recovered him and Emit, right?" Junior asks.

"Elis, the twins, and Zana are all present inside the dining hall."

Junior mutters a string of curses.

"Zeus believes Prende and Chronos made a deal prior to his banishment."

"Did they ever locate her husband Perendi?"

"They believe Perendi caused the earthquake that nearly killed Ana and the one near the City of Time."

"The bastard killed our father! What more does he want?"

"Zeus sent Princess Danae to warn the family of Perendi's involvement."

"Does Zeus know the hourglass Perseus tossed into the ether was fake?" Junior asks.

Dita doesn't answer for a moment. Junior waits for her as she continues to observe the dining hall form the present cavern.

"That question has not come up yet," Dita says. *"Do you think the cavern is secure enough to leave Perseus unattended?"*

"Why?" Junior asks.

"They are making a plan to retrieve the hourglass moments before the earthquake strikes—using the children."

20

Anton mutters, "No, no, no." He furiously paces the floor along the length of the table.

"We can't," Danae says, cuddling Ora. "They were kidnapped just a few hours ago."

"If the hourglass is gone already," Itra says, "then it wasn't Elis. What is there to retrieve?"

"The loop resets the events," Princess Danae says. "We can go through the past ember archway moments before the earthquake and take the hourglass."

Anton stops mid stride. "We?" He points to Elis, who's now hunched over, his head buried in his hands. "You mean my son."

"And time with the divine," Princess Danae says, straightening her posture. "They are all the key and the only way to stop him."

"Stop who?" Anton asks. "From what?"

"If the urtar stone is extracted and not balanced immediately," Princess Danae says, "your worlds cease to exist."

"But they do exist," Anton says, waving his hands around. "So, your theory is shi—crap!"

"Anton," Itra says. "Let's take a moment. We need to gather more information."

Anton rolls his eyes. "I need more than information. I need logic, reason, and truth without riddles!"

"Understood," Princess Danae says.

"It's not just Elis's safety we are concerned about," Danae says. "Trust me, my anxiety is off the charts."

Zana yawns.

"I think we should show the kids the suites," Kaly says, glancing at Anton.

"But..." Emit whines, fighting a yawn, "I don't want to go to bed."

"Kaly's right," Danae says, glancing up at the darkened dome. "I'll take them up now."

Ora climbs down from Danae's lap. She takes Zana's hand and taps Elis's shoulder. "Will you come with us?"

Elis glances at Anton.

Anton nods. "Go ahead, I'll be up soon."

Elis pokes Emit.

Emit pouts.

Elis leans down and whispers, "We can order ice cream with all the toppings."

Emit bolts out of the chair.

Itra shakes his head. "Easy on the sugar promises, Elis."

Elis winks. "Sure uncle."

"Coffee and a shot of whiskey," Xena says.

A clink of cups and small shot glasses appear on the table.

Leon raises the glass of whiskey. "To a plan that will not turn my last brown hair white."

Anton shakes his head. "To a safe plan."

Xena raises her glass. "To a safe plan."

The others raise their glasses and take the shot in one gulp.

Princess Danae coughs. "What is this stuff?"

"Fermented grains aged in oak barrels," Leon says.

"Interesting choice," Princess Danae says, patting her reddening cheeks.

"Back to business," Enyo says. "The vision we saw of Elis in the courtyard with the sundial here in the dining hall over seven years ago is another confirmation that this event happens."

"Can anyone remember the details of the scene?" Leon asks.

A book flies out of the library and drops in the center of the table.

Enyo jumps up and draws her dagger.

"It's just a book," Xena says, lowering Enyo's arm.

The book opens and the pages flip to an illustration.

"The City of Time," Kaly says, running her finger over the caption.

The lights dim in the dining hall.

"What's happening?" Princess Danae asks.

The illustration from the pages fills the room in full scale and three dimensions.

The table and chairs are in the center of a village surrounded by stone buildings and a sandy square.

"It's identical to the square near the market," Princess Danae whispers.

Clusters of people walk around the sundial resting on a stack of stones centered in the courtyard.

A figure in a black cloak appears on the far side of the dining hall.

"Is he real or part of the illusion?" Leon points towards a door to the war room.

"That's the person I saw with the watch," Teuta says, "when I was taken from the City of Time with Prende."

The figure slinks forward, keeping his head low. He slows and circles the sundial.

Kaly and Xena move away from the table.

The others stand, backing away from the table to watch him circle.

96

He places his wrist down on the center of the sundial, and it opens.

An hourglass arises from the center. He removes it and turns it upside down. The movement in the square stops.

"What did he just do?" Deino asks.

The illustration starts to melt and drains into a dark pit on the floor.

The group steps away from the table, getting closer to the walls. They silently watch until the final light of the illustration blinks out.

21

Perseus curls into a ball on the dirt with his back against the boulder that blocks his escape.

"Resigned?" Hermes asks.

Perseus gasps. "What the hell!"

"It suits you," Hermes says, peeking past the rock.

"What does?"

"You, stuck between a rock and a hard place."

"Ha ha," Perseus grumbles. "Did you at least bring water?"

"Nah, just my charming personality."

"Great," Perseus says. "Why did the big guy leave?"

"That's a need to know," Hermes says. "And bro—you will never be part of that club again."

"You're going to regret taking sides," Perseus says.

"Did you forget the last time I picked your side? Our family was tossed out of the Castle of Teskom for your betrayal of Ember."

"My deal with Enyo and her sisters was for my mother's safety," Perseus says.

"Your fake blood oath between Zeus and Phorcys gave everyone pause about the truth," Hermes says, "including a mob of rogue descendants under Poseidon's command."

"You can't be serious," Perseus says.

"The deaths of Poseidon, Medusa, and Athena are all on you buddy!" Hermes shakes his head. "Their deaths and the deaths of Itra's sister Iana."

"Whoa," Perseus says. "It was Enyo's idea. This is not all on me!"

"You had a direct order to take the ember stone to Phorcys as a peace offering," Hermes says, holding up one finger. "One job."

"Says the guy that was the lookout," Perseus says.

"I was a kid!"

"You still are!"

Hermes laughs. "I'm not the one kidnapping innocent children. I'm pretty sure my maturity outweighs your arrogant age."

"My arrogant age, ha! At least I'm not blind."

Hermes mocks Perseus using his hands as talking puppets. "Oh, and what did Hermes not see?"

"Tsk, tsk."

"Oh, come off your high horse," Hermes says. "You're trapped behind a damn rock!"

"I'll tell you if you get me something to drink," Perseus says.

"No thanks," Hermes says. "I'm not that thirsty."

"Bravo," Perseus says and claps. "Your arrogance will get those kids killed."

"My arrogance didn't kidnap them and nearly drop one from the sky!"

"Don't be so dramatic."

"I'm not," Hermes says. "Teuta luckily caught Zana mid fall when I was fighting one of your goons."

"That sounds like it was your fault," Perseus says, "not mine. Plus, divines can fly with or without a cloak."

"I'm sorry," Hermes says, facing the rock. "What do you mean?"

"Usmu," Perseus says. "They protect and carry them."

Hermes turns away. "A giant double-headed bird did not appear in the sky this morning."

"Again, not my fault if she doesn't know how to summon them."

"And I'm arrogant, ha!"

"Did anyone see the figure's arm as he tipped the hourglass?" Kaly asks. "It was marked in gold ink."

"No," Junior says, patting his forearm.

Kaly points towards Princess Danae. "You told Danae that Elis was marked by the keeper's cuff when he was taken seven years ago."

"But Prende's dead, right?" Teuta rubs her forearm. *Don't panic! I can't be marked again. Right?* She twists her wrist from side to side examining her unmarked skin.

Princess Danae nods. "I still have no way of knowing for sure." She taps her forearm. "Perseus was marked as an infant. For children, the mark doesn't appear like it did for Teuta."

"When did it appear?" Xena asks.

"His fourteenth birthday."

"When does Elis turn fourteen?" Xena asks.

"He turned fourteen last month," Anton says, shaking his head. "He doesn't have any marks—that I know of. But Elis and Ora have been having dreams about this place."

Xena points to Junior. "Your mark vanished with the death of Prende, right?"

Junior rolls back his sleeves and holds up his arms. He twists his wrists. "Nothing since the day Hermes daggered Prende's heart." He turns to Leon. "Where is that cuff now?"

"Locked inside the vault," Leon says.

"But could Prende still exist within the time loop?" Kaly asks.

Junior stands and looks from the sisters to Princess Danae. "Have you seen her?"

"Physically seen," Princess Danae says, "no, but I've heard Prende's name in passing."

Junior glares at Enyo. "You know something. Spill it!"

"Pemphredo encountered Prende five years ago," Enyo says. "We began tracking her."

Deino nods. "From what we can tell, she's alive the first five days and gone the last two."

"Gone where?" Junior asks, glowering at Deino.

"Gone as in dead," Deino says.

"Explain," Teuta says, standing and putting a hand on Junior's arm. He shrugs off her affection.

Deino taps the table. "We've seen Prende flying astride an usmu after the loop resets on the second and third day. We've also seen her near the sundial on the fourth day. But on day five, we've seen her husband, Perendi, addressing a group of mourners."

"And on day six, Perendi gathers men near the outskirts of town," Deino says, "for what appears to be a hunting party."

A book flies out of the library.

"Ah!" Anton yelps and ducks as the book grazes his head.

"Sorry," Kaly says, catching the book. "I was just wondering about old funeral traditions." She flips the book over and examines the aged, tattered cover.

The book shakes and opens.

Kaly balances the book as the pages turn. "I wanted to know if the hunting party was a tradition or a threat."

The pages stop moving.

Kaly traces an illustration of men with large knives standing over a wild boar. She sighs in relief. "Tradition."

Enyo rolls her eyes. "Of course, it's tradition," she says. "We are sitting right here. You could have just asked."

Xena glances at Enyo. "Because you and your sister are so forthcoming."

"Do you," Deino asks, waving her hand to the occupied chairs, "or any of you think you could have had a normal life during the last seven years with the knowledge of the time loop?"

Kaly and Itra shake their heads.

"But truth matters," Leon says. "We understand you thought hiding this was for everyone's benefit, but we've been preparing for this day for years. This knowledge was never factored in."

"And the threat of the keeper's cuff had been tabled," Itra says. "Now we have to add this to a growing list of threats to our children."

Princess Danae stands and mirrors Junior's posture. "We need to focus on the cloaked figure accessing the sundial. Is it Elis or someone else?"

Teuta holds up her hand and the dining hall dims once again.

The dark figure appears near the sundial.

Teuta prances over to the figure as he freezes, hand raised over the center of the sundial. "Elis is this tall now," she says.

"Approximately," Itra says, scooting back from the table. He walks closer to inspect the image. "When we saw this the first time, I could see his face." He circles the scene.

Teuta waves her hand, and the image moves in slow motion.

Itra bends level with the figure.

The hood shifts, exposing the profile of a boy.

"Freeze it!" Itra says. "Roll it back two seconds."

Teuta twists her hand counterclockwise.

"There!" Itra says, pointing. "It's definitely Elis." He waves Leon and Anton over.

They stand next to Itra.

"You see that faint white line?" Itra asks, pointing to the boy's cheek.

Anton squints. His eyes find a scar just below the cheekbone. He frowns. "That's definitely the same spot."

"What happened there?" Leon asks. "I've never noticed a scar like that before."

"Glass table versus Elis couch surfing," Anton says. "He was ten. Scared me more than it pained him. The scar is barely visible unless he's super tan."

"What is that on his wrist?" Itra asks, pointing.

Teuta moves her hand and the image rolls forward in slow motion until the wrist is facing Leon and the others.

"It's my watch," Leon says, holding up his wrist to the image, "on timer mode."

Princess Danae walks over to Leon. She points to the sundial. "According to the shadow, it would be five minutes past one in the afternoon."

"And twenty-five minutes on the timer," Leon says.

"We know what time and who," Itra says, "but not why?"

"Danae," Elis whispers.

"Hmm," Danae says, tucking Emit in the bed next to Ora and Zana.

"I know we're all really tired," Elis says, leaning against the door to the suite's living room, "but I need to explain a detail from my dream that may help us decide what to do."

Danae nods and follows Elis into the living area. They take a seat on a purple sofa. "I'm listening."

"I've had this dream a few times," Elis says, fidgeting with the corner of the suede cushion. "Teuta is leading us down into a cave."

"Who is us?" Danae asks.

Elis releases the corner of the cushion. "The twins and Zana are with me and Teuta"

"Ok," Danae says.

"But Teuta falls," Elis says. "I catch her hand, and I try to pull her back up, but she lets go."

Danae rubs her arms. "Can you tell me what you see before you enter the cave or describe what she falls into?"

Elis nods. "When I tip the end of the hourglass, a giant crack appears across the sundial and through the ground. Teuta leads us through there to escape the lightning."

"Lightning," Danae whispers.

Elis sighs. "I know it's all a dream, but based on everything I've heard down there..." He shakes his head. "I think it may be more than a dream."

"I agree," Danae says, scooting closer and wrapping Elis in a hug. "Thank you for telling me. I'll make sure we factor this in when making the plan."

23

Deino scoots her chair away from the dining table and clears her throat as she stands. All eyes turn toward her. "Using Pemphredo's gift of visions, we've put together a rough timeline of events."

Itra, Leon and Anton return to the table.

"Pemphredo has had a recurring dream of a man with a long white beard arriving near dawn."

"Arriving where?" Leon asks.

"Here in the hedge maze," Deino says.

Junior pounds his fist against the table.

Deino raises an eyebrow. "May I continue?"

Junior flares his nostrils. "Of course."

"Great," Deino says. "Xena, we'll need Pem. She can use her gift..."

"More like a curse..." Xena mutters.

"...to become Ora."

"Chronos," Deino says.

"Hell no!" Xena says.

"Hear us out," Enyo says, reaching across the table. "Please."

"You're attempting to comfort me," Xena says. "This can't be good."

Enyo smiles. "It just takes a little warming to melt my icy exterior."

"Hmm," Xena says, tipping up her chin to Deino.

"Leon will use his scythe to open passages to the helix from inside the maze," Deino says. "The twelve passageways will open at dawn."

"Avi will manifest our souls just inside the maze," Enyo says.

Avi grips the ember infinity charm dangling from her necklace, the representation of the soul binding gift bestowed on her during her first visit to the castle.

"Junior and Hermes will support Leon inside the maze if the need arises," Deino says.

"You don't know if that need is warranted?" Leon asks.

"Her vision is limited," Deino says, "but what we do know is that while we are distracted by Chronos's arrival, the children are inside the City of Time."

Kaly opens her mouth.

Deino holds up her hands. "I know how it sounds, but Princess Danae will use her gift to shield the children. No one will notice Elis at the sundial."

"But time doesn't stop in the past," Itra says. "Why do they need to be there?"

"It doesn't stop," Enyo says, "but it can be slowed down. When they enter the City of Time, Ora can slow time before the earthquake begins. A fissure cracks the sundial and exposes the hourglass. It's vital that Elis retrieves the hourglass before the earthquake occurs."

"Elis goes in alone?" Anton asks, leaning forward.

"Princess Danae will be beside him the entire time," Enyo says. "To onlookers she will be out on a stroll with a young lady."

"During the last four weeks," Deino says, "the earthquake happens at twenty after one in the afternoon. But the earthquake has been intensifying over the last two weeks. The first rattle was barely noticeable, but the last one caused damage around the village and lasted for three minutes."

"And we believe that the timing of this earthquake coincides with the attack that killed Prende and Mui seven years ago," Deino says, facing Junior. "Do you recall the time of day when the lightning struck the ground?"

Junior nods. "It was in the afternoon. You think that event causes the earthquake?"

"It's possible," Deino says. "Perendi is capable of moving the earth."

Junior shrugs. "This time loop seems pretty fragile."

"I believe that is why the time is now," Enyo says. "Ember knows that it's cracking."

"Chronos will be here," Kaly asks, "and the kids will be there. What's the endgame here?"

"Teuta, can you bring up the hedge maze?" Enyo asks.

Teuta flicks her wrist, and the room falls dark.

A three-dimensional model of the hedge maze appears in front of Deino. She shifts the model ninety degrees so the others can view the center.

"We believe Chronos will take Pem disguised as Ora and attempt to flee through the passageways of time," Deino says, pointing from the center to an open passage. "Leon will have created a trap near every passage that will lead him inside the helix."

"With Pem?" Xena asks.

"No," Enyo says. "The plan is to have her transform the second they get close to the trap. This distraction will give us enough time to push him through."

Leon laughs. "You think you can just push the God of Time and Space through a trapdoor?"

Enyo stands. "The Protectors of Time have a unique qualification to go up against Chronos." She folds her hands together. "When we are physically linked, we can reflect his power."

"Reflect?" Kaly asks.

"If he attempts to slow or speed up time," Enyo says. "We can counter it."

"How?" Xena asks.

Enyo taps her temple. "It's a mind game."

"Promising," Itra says, shaking his head. "And if your mind game fails?"

"Ember," Deino says. "She's gone up against him before and won."

Kaly holds up a finger. "You want us to risk our children to recover the hourglass, but I've heard no plan regarding when and how they return."

"Pemphredo's vision cuts off the moment the passages are sealed." Enyo studies her hands in her lap. "She can't see beyond that point."

"Does Elis turn the hourglass over in her vision?" Itra asks.

"He does," Enyo says. "And the passages of time close at the exact same moment."

"But you never see the children return to the castle?" Kaly says, glaring at Enyo.

"Not exactly," Deino says.

Anton and Kaly throw up their hands.

Leon snarls at Enyo. "You lied to us."

"I never lied!" Enyo glares at Leon. "Pemphredo has zero control over the visions."

Itra holds up his hands. "Ana mentioned she watched the sand fall from the hourglass into a cupped hand." He forms his hand in a cup and then splays his fingers flattening his hand. "The sand falls freely leaving only the stone."

"I'll repeat what I heard when I touched the Anubis scale in the vault," Enyo says. "Stack the stone against your own. A compass to guide is near inside. To begin again or tip the end. You must decide."

"Enough with the riddles," Anton says. He scoots his chair back from the table. "Just explain it. Are the kids safe or not?"

Enyo and Deino exchange a glance.

108

"We don't honestly know," Enyo says, staring down at the table.

"Hold on," Xena says. "Let's examine what we know. Chronos will be here, and the children will be inside the City of Time with Princess Danae."

Princess Danae nods. "And under the protection of Zeus."

Kaly shakes her head. "But we don't know if Prende or Perendi are a threat."

"Wrong," Danae says, walking into the dining hall.

Itra whirls to look Danae over. Her frown has him up and out of his chair. "What is it?"

"Elis confirmed that there is a threat inside the City of Time," Danae says, hugging Itra.

Anton stands. "What do you mean?"

Danae releases Itra and walks to the table. "They flee the courtyard after he tips the hourglass because of lightning."

"Perendi," Deino says.

"I believe so," Danae says.

"But do they get away?" Enyo asks.

"Teuta leads them into a cave to escape," Danae says, turning to find Teuta, "but she falls, leaving the kids alone."

"I fall?" Teuta asks. "How?"

"Elis says he tries to help you," Danae says, biting the corner of her bottom lip. "But—"

"But what?" Junior asks.

Anton says, "She lets go."

Junior glares at Anton.

Anton shakes his head. "Elis has been drawing parts of his dreams for weeks. He's shown me the drawing."

Kaly stands and walks towards the library door.

"Where are you going?" Junior asks.

"If there is an answer," Kaly says without pausing, "we have less than twelve hours to find it."

"She's right," Xena says. "I'll head to the present cavern and check in with Dita and Pem." She jogs towards the conservatory door.

"Logistically," Itra says. "I don't hear a safe passage for the kids. Who besides Teuta and her," he says, pointing to Princess Danae, "are going with the children?"

"If you think I am letting them out of my sight," Danae says, "you're very wrong."

Enyo looks to Deino.

Deino shrugs. "I don't have a problem with it."

Leon laughs. "That wasn't a request."

24

"Hermes," Perseus whispers. "Are you still there?"

Hermes ignores him. He dangles his feet over the edge of the cavern and stares down at the moon's reflection rippling in the shallows of the lake.

"He's coming," Perseus says.

Distant thunder rumbles and echoes inside the cavern.

Hermes scoots back from the edge.

"Leave, fly boy!" Perseus shouts. "He's close!"

Hermes stands. "What are you talking about?"

"Perendi!" Perseus shouts, punching the rock. "Leave now! Save yourself!"

Thunder claps and the sky streaks with blue light.

Hermes ducks his head. "Why is Perendi coming here?"

"He's working with Chronos!" Perseus says. "Go!"

"You knew Chronos had allies?"

"Please, just go!"

The ground rattles as another bout of thunder rolls overhead.

"He'll kill you," Perseus whispers. "Please, go!"

Hermes steps closer to the edge. He winces as lightning strikes the lake below. He rubs the hair standing on his neck.

A silhouette of a man appears in the clouds shading the moon.

"If you betray Ember or those kids," Hermes says, "I will make sure you pay for it!"

"I know!" Perseus says.

Hermes nose dives out of the cavern.

A man emerges from the clouds.

Hermes hides under an overhanging rock and hovers. He watches Perendi approach the cavern opening.

"Perseus," Perendi says, pausing outside of the cave.

"I swear by this thunder-stone," Perseus says. "That I have not stolen it nor has any one of my house. I don't know who stole it! If I am lying to you, may a bolt strike me!"

"Did I accuse you?" Perendi asks, tilting his head to the side and landing just inside the cave.

"Sorry," Perseus says. "Are you here to release me or kill me?"

Perendi laughs. The sound of his laughter echoes, shaking the entire cliff side.

Hermes dodges a few large rocks hurtling towards him.

"We can't keep him waiting," Perendi says.

The boulder trapping Perseus explodes into a billion pieces.

Perseus shields his face.

Hermes flies up above the cavern opening to avoid the debris.

Perseus coughs as the dust settles around him. He wipes his eyes and finds Perendi standing in the middle of the rubble dust free and smiling.

Perendi winks at Perseus. "Now then, what were you saying?"

Perseus spits out the dirt lining the inside of his mouth. "Are you going to kill me?"

"I should, but Chronos has other plans."

Hermes flies higher landing on the clearing above the cavern. He can still hear the conversation below.

"Does he have my wife?" Perseus asks, glaring at Perendi.

"Maybe," Perendi says, bumping his wrists together.

Perseus glances down at his own wrists, which are suddenly bound in a gold rope. He tugs against the restraints and the rope tightens.

"Is this really necessary?" Perseus says, holding up his hands.

Perendi reaches forward. A piece of the rope lengthens and extends.

"A lead, really?" Perseus asks.

Perendi smirks, gripping the end of the rope. He yanks Perseus forward.

Perseus makes it two steps and slams his head against an invisible barrier. "What the—"

Perendi tugs on the rope again with more force.

Perseus crashes against something again. It knocks him off balance, and he falls to his knees.

Perendi rushes forward but is bounced back. "Impossible!" He reaches out until his hand finds the barrier. His palm tingles. He inspects the rope that is breaking through it. He tugs on the rope, swinging it up and down.

Perseus pulls on the rope, smashing Perendi's face against the barrier. "Ha! How's that for karma?"

Perendi takes a step back and raises his arms, releasing the rope from his grasp.

Perseus hastily gets to his feet. He backs away from Perendi's snarling face.

"Ember thinks she can best me?" Perendi asks. The veins around his neck bulge and his face reddens. "Try this!" He swings his arms down and a bolt of lightning bursts out of him.

Perseus cowers back, covering his face.

"Ah!" Perendi yells as the energy bounces back, slamming him in the chest. The force propels him out of the cavern.

Hermes watches Perendi's limp body pinwheel in an arc spiraling towards the lake. He smashes into the lake with a hiss of steam.

Hermes flies down into the cavern.

Perseus blinks as the ropes fall from his wrists.

"What happened?" Hermes asks, stepping over the rubble.

"Ember stopped him from taking me," Perseus says, pressing a hand against the invisible barrier.

"Where was he taking you?" Hermes asks, poking the barrier.

"To Chronos," Perseus says. "They were using me to get inside and take time."

25

Danae and Avi join Kaly in the library.

"Any luck?" Danae asks, leaning over Kaly's shoulder and reading the blue cursive text on the page.

"Not anything useful," Kaly says. "But I've just begun." She nods to a stack of books set on a table in the center of the small library. "Take one."

Avi picks up the first book and thumbs through the pages. She pauses on the last entry and studies the text.

Kaly closes a book and takes another. "I might have a solution for the keeper's cuff."

"I'm listening," Danae says.

"If Elis were to become the keeper of the cuff," Kaly says, "the mark made by Prende would be essentially obsolete."

"No," Danae says. "That would be a life sentence."

Kaly shakes her head. "It's a solution with no consequence."

"What do you mean?" Avi asks.

"If Elis never uses the cuff on anyone," Kaly says, "it's not a burden to carry."

Danae sighs.

Kaly bumps Danae's shoulder. "We can run it by Anton."

Itra sticks his head in the door. "I'm heading up to check on the kids and Anton."

"Can you send Anton down?" Danae asks.

"Sure," Itra says, stepping closer to Danae. "We'll need sleep soon."

"I know," Danae says, rolling to her toes to kiss him on the cheek. "Soon."

Itra nods. He steps out of the library and bumps into Hermes. "Whoa, when did you get back?"

"Now," Hermes says. "Perendi attempted to take Perseus, but Ember stopped him." He looks around the hall and immediately dips his head in a bow. "Princess Danae."

"Hermes," Princess Danae says, walking over to the gathering crowd.

Junior towers over Hermes. "Explain."

Hermes uses his hands to mime a wall. "There is an invisible barrier trapping Perseus inside the cavern."

"Like the one guarding the opening in the present cavern?" Itra asks.

Hermes nods. "Perendi used his power of earth to obliterate the boulder blocking Perseus and bound his wrists with a gold rope. But he couldn't pull Perseus out of the cavern. He used his old standby, lightning, but the barrier held, pushing the lightning bolt back at him. It knocked him out of the cavern and into the lake."

"He's dead?" Danae asks.

"No," Hermes says. "Not likely, but I didn't see him emerge from the water."

"Can you summon Pemphredo?" Princess Danae asks Avi.

Avi nods. She pulls out the gold chain from under her top and holds the ember infinity charm.

Enyo and Deino each lay a hand on Avi's shoulders.

Avi closes her eyes and furrows her brow.

Pemphredo appears in a dark red cloak to the left of Enyo.

"Why the worried faces?" Pemphredo asks, taking in the group.

"Have you seen Perendi this evening?" Enyo asks.

"He's running towards the grottos as we speak." Pemphredo turns to Enyo. "Why?"

"Perendi attempted to take Perseus as an errand boy for Chronos," Hermes says.

"What is in the grottos?" Avi asks.

Deino glances at Enyo. "The ley lines converge in the center of the grottos—below the sundial."

A book flies off the shelf nearly colliding with Danae, and hovers in front of Kaly.

"Sorry," Kaly says, taking the book. "I read that the City of Time was built on ancient ley lines."

Enyo nods.

"At any intersection of ley lines is a supposedly a portal," Kaly says, holding up her thumb adorned with the gold ring. "Like our rings. According to folklore, the portals are often mystified by fairies and witches." She catches Leon's frown as he joins the crowd. "But research at a few stone circles found variance of time inside the intersection of known ley lines."

"I've seen this intersection," Deino says. "And I believe that if you were to draw a line between the fairy statue in the center of the hedge maze here in the castle to sea level, it would align with the sundial in the City of Time."

"A portal," Danae whispers. "That's how Chronos will access the castle."

Every eye turns towards the door leading to the conservatory and the stairwells overlooking the hedge maze.

A collective shudder runs through the group.

Leon turns to Teuta. "Is there a mechanism or fancy item from the vault that can counter a portal opening from the ley lines?"

"Not that I know of," Teuta says. "We can look, but there something I need to do first." She closes her eyes and chants. "Illyria ember in time, light the fire to inspire."

All eyes shift to Teuta.

Leon sways from side to side. "Why do I feel like I just got flooded with adrenaline?"

Teuta smirks. "Sleep is overrated!"

"Says the fairy that knocked us out our first night here," Itra says, shaking out the urge to run.

Teuta rolls her eyes. "Just the messenger!"

Kaly holds two fingers to her neck. "My pulse is pounding."

"It's completely safe," Teuta says, waving her hand.

Danae shakes her head. "Did this little spell work on the children too?"

Teuta's smile falls and her jaw drops open.

"Are you kidding me?" Danae yells.

"Sorry," Teuta says, backing away from the group.

"I give you permission to do your worst," Danae says, poking Leon in the chest. "I'm going to check on the kids."

Danae marches out of the dining hall.

Leon cracks his neck and lunges towards Teuta.

"Hey!" Teuta yelps, disappearing and reappearing behind Junior.

"She's just trying to help," Junior says, holding Leon back.

Xena and Pem run in from the conservatory.

"Why do I feel like I just drank eighty shots of espresso?" Pem asks.

Everyone but Junior points to Teuta.

Xena steps between Junior and Leon. "We have bigger priorities at the moment."

Teuta whispers, "Thank you."

"Don't thank me yet," Xena says, glaring at her. "We need access to the archives and the vault to prepare." She folds her arms across her chest. "Does Ember give us free access?"

Teuta tilts her chin up and meets her glare. "Of course."

"Great," Xena says, pushing Leon and Junior towards the conservatory door. "We have less than seven hours. Take the first watch in the towers. And Hermes head back to Perseus."

"Who made you boss?" Junior asks, pausing at the door.

Xena lifts an eyebrow. "I wasn't aware your ego was at stake. Would you like to give orders or take action?"

Leon stifles a laugh.

Xena cuts him a look.

Leon grins.

"Just go," Xena says. "We'll send up relief in a few hours."

Junior and Leon follow Hermes out of the dining hall.

Xena sighs and turns back to the group. She approaches Pemphredo. "Have you seen Andromeda since this morning?"

"No," Pemphredo answers. "Is she missing?"

"She was expelled by Ember," Enyo says. "You haven't seen her sulking about?"

"No," Pemphredo says. "I'll reach out and see if anyone has seen her."

Avi releases her charm and Pemphredo vanishes.

"We'll head down to the archives," Enyo says, gesturing to Deino. "Hopefully, we'll find a way to block the portal from the ley lines."

Xena nods. Teuta waves her hand, and the sisters vanish.

"Itra," Kaly says. "We need the keeper's cuff from the vault. Take Pem, but please handle it with care."

"Do you think we should run this past Anton first?" Avi asks.

Itra whirls. "The cuff is for Elis?"

"It's just a precaution to counter Prende if a mark appears on Elis," Kaly says. "We only want to be prepared."

"I'll continue to look through the books up here with Kaly," Avi says.

Itra and Pem nod before vanishing from the dining hall.

26

Andromeda's knees shake under the strain of her frozen stance. *How long can he leave me like this?* She attempts to blink but fails. *Seriously!*

A shadow crosses the doorway, followed by a scuffle of footsteps and heavy panting.

"Where is he!" Chronos shouts.

"Emb—" a man starts to say.

"Don't you dare say her name!" Chronos shouts.

"She protected him," the man says, catching his breath.

"You useless excuse for a god!" Chronos bellows.

"How dare you!" the man shouts back.

"You are a fool to think our alliance will ever bring your dead wife back to life!"

The ragged hair remaining on Andromeda's head lifts just before a flash of light blinds her eyes.

"Fool," Chronos says.

"Help me," the man whispers.

Chronos laughs. His chuckle draws closer to Andromeda.

I can't see!

"It appears," Chronos says, flicking her forehead.

Andromeda's body reanimates and she falls to her knees. She rubs her eyes and gasps.

"You're my only bait," Chronos says, nudging her shoulder with his foot.

"What?" Andromeda says between breaths.

"Ember has your precious husband, and I have his only heir."

Andromeda wraps her arm around her waist. "You know?"

"Why, yes." Chronos kneels to her level. "If something happens to you, Ember's legacy of time never exists."

Andromeda makes out his form, but none of his features. "Then why are we still alive?" She rubs her eyes.

"Because she will expect that," Chronos says, standing and stepping beside her. He tugs her up.

Andromeda wobbles and attempts to pull away.

"And where do you expect to go?" Chronos asks, tightening his grip.

Andromeda spits in his face. "I would rather die than play your game."

"That's kind," Chronos says, smiling. "But not now."

"What is your end game anyway?" Andromeda asks.

"Not an end, but a new beginning."

27

Itra lands next to Pem. "It's normally my stomach turns upside down." He rubs his temple. "Why is my head pounding?"

Pem scrunches her nose. "Portaling plus the adrenaline boost?"

Itra nods, looking up and down the towering endless line of the random collection of artifacts, chests, framed art, statues, vehicles, and various aircrafts. "You've spent more time down here than I have. Do you know where—"

Pem holds up a leather pouch and shakes it. "It's thought provoked."

Itra reaches out to still her hand. "Let's handle that with a bit more care."

"Sorry," Pem says. "Teuta, beam us back to the dining hall."

"Wait," Itra says.

"What is it?" Pem asks, looking around.

"There's someone else down here," Itra whispers, lifting his chin towards a tall, red case.

Pem pockets the leather pouch. She taps her mirror charm and transforms into Enyo. She pulls a dagger out of her back shoulder harness and slowly advances. "We know you're in here. Come out slowly with your hands raised over your head."

Ora peeks her head around the case. "Hi daddy."

"Ora, sweetheart, what are you doing out of bed? And how did you get down here?" Itra runs towards her.

Ora meets him halfway and launches herself into his arms. "I'm not dreaming?"

Itra pats her back. "No, darlin'."

Pem slides the dagger back into the harness before transforming back to herself.

"Pem!" Ora shrills. "How did you do that?"

Pem winks. "Magic."

Ora pulls back and frowns at Itra. "Dad, did you know Pem could do magic?"

"Yes," Itra says, looking over Ora's shoulder at Pem. "It's just a little thing she can do."

"Pish!" Ora shakes her head. "That's not little, dad!" She holds out her hands as wide as they will go. "That's huge!"

"Ok, you got me," Itra says, grinning. "You can tell your mom all about it."

Ora wiggles and claps. "She doesn't know?"

"Oh, she'll be surprised alright."

Pem drags a finger out from the tip of her nose but drops her hand when Ora turns towards her.

Itra laughs.

"Why did you think you were dreaming?" Pem asks.

Ora tilts her head to the side. "It was Ember. I think. She kept repeating the phrase, 'find the scale or fail'." She points to a gold scale a few feet away. "And I woke up here."

Pem walks to the scale. "This one?"

Ora nods. "Yep!"

"This is the Anubis scale," Pem says.

Itra nods. "Can you pick it up?"

Pem hesitantly reaches for the scale.

"Stop," Ora says. She wiggles down from Itra's grasp. "You'll need help."

Pem turns to Ora. "Did you try to pick it up?"

Ora shakes her head. "It has to be balanced."

"How do you know that?" Pem asks.

Ora shrugs. "I just know."

Pem looks at Itra.

"You heard her," Itra says, stepping to one side of the gold scale.

Pem nods. "Ok, on three. One, two, three."

Itra and Pem lift the scale carefully off the marble dais.

Ora smiles. "That's great." She turns and looks around. "Are there stairs or something?"

"Or something," Pem says. "Teuta, we have Ora and a scale."

⚖️

Itra and Pem land inside the Zeus war room.

Ora appears a second later.

Danae swoops Ora up in a hug.

"Mom, I can't breathe," Ora squeaks.

"You scared us to death," Danae says. "Where were you?"

Itra and Pem gently set the scale on the table.

"We found her in the vault," Itra says, wiping a falling tear from Danae's cheek. "She's fine."

Danae loosens her hug and looks at Ora. "How did you end up in the vault?"

"Ember sent me to find a scale," Ora says. "I thought it was a dream." She cups her hands around Danae's ear and leans in. "But I saw Pem do magic."

"Oh, is that right?" Danae says, fighting to keep her face neutral.

Ora places a finger over her lips. "Shh."

Danae drags two fingers across her lips and twists at the corner. She takes the imaginary key and hands it to Ora.

Ora giggles.

"Ora!" Emit shouts, running at full speed towards Danae.

Elis and Zana follow Emit, close on his heels. Emit crashes into Danae's side and she bumps into the table.

Itra and Pem rush forward. Itra palms the dangling saucer before it crashes to the table. Pem gently pulls on the other saucer. The scale slowly levels back out.

Elis points to the scale. "Is that what made you get out of bed?"

Ora nods. "You had the same dream?"

"Yes," Elis says, running a hand through his curly hair. "But I couldn't wake up."

Ora wiggles out of Danae's embrace and hugs Elis around his waist. "It's ok."

Xena, Anton, and Kaly run into the room.

"She's back," Anton says, breathless. "We heard Emit shout and..."

"She's ok," Itra says, patting Anton on the shoulder.

Anton sighs and bends at the waist. "This is too much."

"We should call off the search," Kaly says, hugging Zana.

"We heard she's back," Avi says, walking in with Princess Danae.

Enyo appears in the war room next to Avi and points at the scale. "What is that doing up here?" She grips the hilt of the sword at her hip and scans the room.

Princess Danae steps between the table and Enyo. "It's time."

"No," Enyo says, shaking her head. "It can't be."

"What is she talking about?" Kaly asks.

Princess Danae turns to face Kaly. "The prophecy." She looks over at Elis. "Move the scale and fail. To balance again, he must tip the end."

"Who is 'he' in the prophecy?" Itra asks.

"Elis," Princess Danae says.

Anton steps in front of Elis. "What are you saying?" he asks.

"A day will come when this world is one," Princess Danae says. "A divine bride will lead the guide inside to begin again. He must tip the end."

Teuta appears and says, "Four worlds will bend and fold to derive a world untold."

"You knew about this?" Itra asks, pointing a finger at Teuta and then the scale.

"Of course," Teuta says. "That's why the scale was kept in the vault."

124

"You appear and stop us from doing shi..." Pem catches Zana's wide-eyed expression, "stuff all the time. Why play dumb now?"

Teuta tilts her head to the side. "Play dumb?"

Kaly shakes her head. "Idiot!"

Itra towers over Teuta. "You wanted us to fail!"

"I'm the messenger," Teuta says. "If Ember wanted me to intervene, I would have."

"Ember!" Kaly says, snapping. "What if Ember is the divine bride? It was their failed courtship that banished Chronos to the helix, right?"

A book flies past Teuta and hovers in front of Kaly.

"What is it?" Xena asks.

The thin old book opens with a puff of dust.

Kaly staggers back and holds her breath. She steps only close enough to read the cursive handwriting. "To end your reign, I break my vow. To start again, you must bow. Until then, it ends with me. By my line, I banish thee, time, to the helix for infinity."

The scale saucers start twirling in opposite directions.

Enyo lays a finger on the center of the scale and jerks her hand away. "He's screaming!"

The saucers spin faster.

"I don't hear anything," Ora says.

Danae leans down and whispers, "Enyo's special gift is hearing objects."

Ora rolls to her toes. "Really?"

Danae nods.

"Enyo," Kaly says. "What did he say?"

Enyo swallows back a sob. "He's here."

28

Leon paces around the glass tower scouring the land around the castle. *"Do you see anything?"* He leans his forehead against the cool glass.

"No," Junior answers, looking over at the other tower. *"Are you pacing?"*

Leon pauses long enough to glare over at Junior in the other tower.

The clouds part. The full moon bathes the castle in a new light.

Leon's eyes focus on the fairy statue holding the stone heads of Athena and Medusa in the center of the hedge maze far below. The shadows of the hedges create a dark halo around the figure.

"I can't see the entire hedge maze from here," Leon says. *"I'm going down to walk around the parapet."*

"I'll stay here and keep my eyes on the sky," Junior says.

Leon walks down the spiral steps. He taps his ember staff and leans it forward to light his path over the smooth, worn stone.

The cool evening breeze glides over his neck. He shrugs off the chill and picks up his pace.

"Leon!" Kaly shouts.

Leon stops walking and looks down over the edge of the parapet. *"Kaly! Where are you?"*

"He's here!"

Leon spots a large figure shimmer into existence in the middle of the hedge maze. He blinks twice. *No, that's real!*

A long white beard glows in the moonlight. The man turns and tilts his head up.

Leon releases his staff, extinguishing the light and backing away from the parapet edge. He races towards the stairs. *"Junior!"*

"What is it?" Junior asks.

"He's here!" Leon says breathlessly as he descends another flight of steps.

"Now?" Junior asks, looking out of the tower. *"Where?"*

"Hedge maze!" Leon skids to a stop on the first-floor landing. He creeps up to the large window. He peers out at the man circling the fairy statue. "He's laughing," he says to himself.

"Who is?" Kaly says, climbing the steps to the landing. Leon holds up his hand, palm out. Kaly pauses her ascent.

"Chronos is poking the stone head of Medusa," Leon says, flattening his body against the wall. "I think he finds it amusing."

"What do we do?" Kaly asks.

"He's early," Leon says, shaking his head. "I didn't set any of the portal traps. Where are the kids?"

"Teuta transported them to the archive suite with Princess Danae and Anton," Kaly says.

Leon nods and takes another look. He catches movement in the window directly across from him. *"Junior."*

"I've got eyes on him," Junior says. *"Go to the others. Figure out a plan. I'll send word if he attempts to escape the maze."*

"Don't do anything stupid!" Leon says, risking another look. The man has his back to him. Leon bolts past the window and takes Kaly's hand. "Let's go to the others. Junior will keep watch."

Kaly squeezes his hand. "Avi summoned Pemphredo. She hasn't responded."

"She was supposed to be our eyes and ears in the City of Time," Leon says, jogging down the steps and through the conservatory.

Kaly keeps up with his pace. "Trust me, I know. Enyo and Deino are not happy. Avi, Pem, and Xena are in the archives to find an alternative way to keep him in the maze for now."

Leon and Kaly rush into the dining hall.

Enyo whirls with her sword out.

"Whoa," Kaly says, stopping mid stride.

"Sorry," Enyo says, sliding her sword back into its sheath. "Pemphredo finally answered. Zeus has men out looking for Andromeda."

"No one has seen her?" Kaly asks.

"Not since yesterday," Enyo says. "And Perendi was spotted near the entrance of the grottos. He's in pretty bad shape."

"Well then," Leon says. "Hopefully, he won't be a threat."

"The loop resets in thirty minutes," Deino says. "We really need to get the hourglass before the damage occurs to the sundial."

"In every scenario," Danae says, "it's never been at night. Why the rush now?"

"If they leave now, they might make it," Deino says, pointing up. The moon is directly over the center of the dome. "Chronos is speeding up time."

The moon abruptly falls out of view. The dark sky lightens to a grey blue.

"Something's happening!" Junior shouts. *"The sun is... spinning!"*

29

"Oh Ember," Chronos says, circling the fairy statue. "I'm here my love."

"Leave now and spend eternity free," Ember sings.

Chronos looks up. "Alone?"

"With your favorite person, of course."

He glances behind him. "Oh. Is that supposed to be a joke?"

"You were always obsessed with just one person," she whispers from beside him.

Chronos turns with his hand out but only finds the fairy statue staring back. "Come out and have this conversation in person," he says. "It's been centuries."

"But for you, it's only been days."

He smirks. "You know about the loop," he says.

"Goddess of Knowledge, remember."

"Ha, I'll never forget," Chronos says, stroking his long white beard. "I've been waiting for this day."

"To best me?"

"To win your affection," he says, putting a hand over his heart.

"Ha."

"I can be quite persuasive."

"Conniving is a better word for what you can be."

He whirls as the breath of her last word buzzes over his ear. "My only goal is to reign with you by my side."

"You would share... in your tyranny. How profound."

He pouts. "You mock my sincere plea?"

"Do you think me a fool?"

"By my word, never," he says.

"Your word," Ember scoffs, "means nothing."

"Please, let me show you with my actions," Chronos says, waving his right hand.

The rapid speed of time slows, and the sun peeks out of the cloud cover.

Junior risks a look out. The sun beams over the hedge maze illuminating the figure. Chronos looked solid in the moonlight, but he now appears translucent. *He's not physically here.*

"Leon," Junior says, *"it's almost noon. And he's not real."*

"What do you mean?" Leon asks, jogging towards the conservatory door.

"I can see through him," Junior says.

Leon stops, nearly crashing into a row of plants. "Teuta."

Teuta appears ahead of him.

"Is Chronos an illusion or a threat?" Leon asks, walking towards her.

Teuta wipes the beads of sweat off her brow. "I believe a threat, but Ember has asked us not to interfere until she commands."

Leon narrows his eyes. "Why are you staring at my face like you've seen a ghost?"

"His manipulation of time was more than just hours," Teuta says. She points to the basin below the sculpted elephant water fountain.

Leon steps closer and peers down at his reflection. He runs a hand over a bristly white beard attached to an older version of himself. "What the—" He inspects the new wrinkles across his forehead and the lines creasing his once chiseled face.

"How many years?" Leon whispers.

"Decades," a woman says.

Leon whirls to face a tall, slender woman. Her oval face and emerald eyes resemble only one person.

His mouth falls open. "Zana?"

30

"Hermes," Dita says, watching the sky flicker from day to night through the opening in the present cavern.

Hermes walks away from Perseus. *"What's up?"*

"Chronos is here inside the maze!"

"No!" Hermes says, turning back towards Perseus. "Chronos is inside the castle."

Perseus stands. "How?"

"How did he get in?" Hermes asks, pacing between the barrier and the cavern opening.

"He just appeared in the middle of the hedge maze."

"Had they set the trap?"

"No, he was early."

"Hermes!" Perseus yells.

Hermes turns and his mouth falls open.

Perseus is hunched over, and his face is lined with new wrinkles. "What's happening?" He pulls his hair forward, watching it go grey before his very eyes.

"Dita!" Hermes panics. *"Perseus is—um—aging."*

"Hold on," Dita says, staring at Perseus through the live feed. *"Junior, what's going on up there?"*

"Can you see the sky?" Junior asks Dita.

"Of course," Dita says, walking back to the edge. *"It's been flickering dark to light since you said Chronos arrived."*

"He's talking to someone," Junior says. "I'm assuming Ember and him are chatting."

"Have you noticed anything else?" Dita asks. She looks over her own hands. The skin appears thin and spotted. *What is happening?*

"Dita!" Hermes says.

"It's not safe here, Hermes," Dita says. "Use your ring and return home."

"But what about Perseus?" Hermes asks, shaking his head.

"Leave him," Dita says. "Go, and Hermes, don't use the Ember archways until you find Pemphredo or Princess Danae."

⚖

Hermes walks into his suite inside the City of Time. He rushes to the balcony. The murmur of the crowd below draws his attention towards the market. He spots Pemphredo running through the crowd. She looks back over her shoulder. A large man is following her, pushing people out of the way.

Hermes tightens his tunic and jumps from the balcony. He soars over the crowds, reaching Pemphredo. He lands beside her at a run.

"Why are you running?" Hermes asks, looking over his shoulder.

"Hermes!" Pemphredo checks over her shoulder. "Why are you here?" She yanks him into a small alley and takes an immediate right down a flight of stairs. She shoves a door open and drags Hermes inside.

"What's going on?" Hermes asks, catching his breath.

"Perendi's men," Pemphredo says, latching the door shut with an iron pin. "They've been chasing me for hours."

"Why?" Hermes asks.

"Chronos and Perendi had a bit of a falling out," Pemphredo says, placing her ear against the door. "Why did you return?"

"Chronos is inside the Castle of Teskom."

"What?"

"That's not the worst part."

Pemphredo faces Hermes.

"He's done something with time," Hermes says, patting his cheek. "I was with Perseus when Chronos arrived, and shortly after, Perseus started rapidly aging."

"No," Pemphredo says, slumping to the ground. "I need to get my sisters out of there. Where were the kids?"

"I didn't ask," Hermes says. "Dita told me to leave and not return through the ember archways. Can you reach Avi?"

Pemphredo shakes her head.

Hermes holds up his thumb with the gold ring. "We can use this."

Pemphredo nods.

Hermes concentrates his thoughts on the dining hall inside the Castle of Teskom. *Protect time, unite to fight. Ember of mine.*

A door appears as he reaches for it, it disappears.

Hermes tries again. *Protect time, unite to fight. Ember of mine.*

A door appears for a second and then disappears again.

"What's wrong?" Pemphredo asks.

"Protect time," Hermes says aloud, "unite to fight. Ember of mine."

Pemphredo turns slowly around.

"Something's wrong!" Hermes mutters.

31

"Hi dad," Zana says. "The white beard kind of suits you."

"It can't be," Leon says. "You're seven!"

"More like thirty-seven," Zana says, going to him.

"No, no, no!" Leon says, shaking his head. "We can fix this!"

"Dad," Zana says, wrapping her arms around him. "We tried."

"What?" Leon asks, leaning away from her. "How?"

"Come," Zana says, looping an arm around him. "The others are waiting." She holds the dining hall door open for Leon.

Kaly turns and Leon's knees buckle.

"Leon!" Kaly says, running towards him.

Zana holds him up. Kaly wraps her arm around him. They walk him to the table.

Leon slumps into a chair and looks across the table at Danae. Her swollen, red eyes are looking despondently at the table.

"Sis," Leon whispers.

Danae sniffles and looks up at him. Her short dark hair is streaked with silver and the worry crease between her brow has deepened. She cocks her head at him and says, "You look like Uncle Steve."

"Holy shit," Leon says, shaking his head. "I knew the reflection looked familiar." He looks over her shoulder at Itra's shiny bald head. "What's happened?"

"When Chronos arrived," Enyo says, "he hit the accelerator button on our present timetable."

"But Junior said the man in the hedge maze isn't actually a man!" Leon says, pointing towards the door.

"It's enough of him to cause the damage you've seen," Enyo says.

Zana lays a hand on Leon's shoulder, and he catches the glint of a diamond. He grabs her hand and examines the ring on her left ring finger. "You're married?"

A man clears his throat to Leon's left.

Leon turns and looks the man up and down. "Elis?"

"Yes sir," Elis says, holding up his left hand with a gold band. "I hope we have your blessing."

"Whoa," Leon says, holding his chest. "Back way up! Tell me how the hell all of this happened." He looks at his watch. "In the span of the last hour, the children were in the archives." He points at Zana and Elis. "Not only have you aged, but you're also married? Where the hell was I?"

"We never made it to the archives," Zana says, sitting between Elis and Leon.

"Ember booted us out with Princess Danae," a man with a deep voice says, sitting down next to Danae. "And Anton..."

"Emit?" Leon says.

"Present," Emit says, holding up his hand.

Leon gapes at the similarity between Itra and Emit.

Emit smiles, seeming to read his thoughts. "What can I say? Like father, like son." He pats his head. "But thanks to your side of the family I still have hair."

Itra frowns. "Ha ha."

"Where did you guys end up?" Leon asks, looking around the table. "Wait, where's Ora?"

Emit sucks in a ragged breath. "Ora's in the archives helping with the research but as to where we ended up, well we'll get to that." He nods to Zana.

136

Zana straightens and takes Elis's hand. "We ended up inside the City of Time." She nods towards Teuta. "It's probably easier to show you."

The dining hall light stone dims and a scene appears of Elis, Zana, Ora, and Emit as they were before time sped up.

"Where are we?" Elis says, kneeling in the grass. He checks on Zana and Ora.

Princess Danae leans over and whispers, "Turn around."

Emit points at the cliff side.

"I've been here," Elis whispers.

Princess Danae nods. "This is the City of Time."

"Wow," Ora says.

Zana points up to a large, white stone building protruding from the cliff side overlooking the stone buildings below. "Is that a castle?"

Princess Danae smiles. "It's my home."

Emit rolls his eyes. "Just call it what it is." He points. "That's a castle."

"Fine," Princess Danae says, holding up her hands. "It's a castle."

"Where's my dad?" Elis asks.

"I'm assuming Ember had other plans for him," Princess Danae says, pointing towards Pemphredo. "She may know what's happening?"

Pemphredo approaches, nodding to Princess Danae and giving Ora and Zana a wink. "Hi, I was not expecting the five of you."

"We were sent to the archives but landed here," Princess Danae says.

"Are my sisters escorting you?" Pemphredo looks around her.

"No," Princess Danae says. "Can you reach Avi?"

"Hermes and I have been trying to reach the others inside the castle." She gestures to the city gates. "We should get to the hourglass." She looks around. "Did you bring the ruby and the scale?"

"No, why?" Elis asks.

"They are the only way to balance the urtar stone," Pemphredo says. Her face goes a little pale. "We'll have to be sure to not tip the end until we return to the Castle of Teskom."

"Elis," Princess Danae says. "Are you ok?"

Elis nods. "I think so. Why?"

"You're sweating through your shirt," Emit says, pointing to the dark patches under his arms and on his chest.

"Just nervous," Elis whispers.

Ora steps beside Elis. "We'll be right by your side."

"No!" Elis says. "You three have to stay out of the city."

"I don't think they are safe here," Pemphredo says. "Perendi may be injured, but he is causing a great deal of damage inside and outside of the city."

Elis shakes out his hands. "This is just like my dream."

Ora nods. "I know." She takes his hand. "We have to go right now." She points up at the sun. "It's nearly at high noon."

Zana tugs Pemphredo's hand. "Can you get word to our parents that we are here?"

"I'll keep trying," Pemphredo says. "Keep them close and shield them."

Princess Danae nods. "Where are you going?"

"Hermes gave Perendi's men something to chase out of the city walls." She looks over her shoulder. "But there are still men looking for me. I'll keep trying to reach my sisters and find an alternative to balance the urtar stone without the scale."

The princess nods. "Zana and Ora walk in front of me. Emit and Elis follow behind me. And no matter what happens do not leave my side!" She looks each one in the eyes. "Nod if you understand."

138

The four of them nod and take their positions.

Princess Danae directs Ora and Zana inside a small passage and up a flight of stairs to an open courtyard. They march together as a group into the crowd of villagers milling through market and darting in and out of buildings.

Ora hesitates, but Princess Danae nudges her forward.

"Walk tall and with purpose," Princess Danae whispers to Zana and Ora.

The little girls straighten their tiny frames and march forward. The crowd immediately responds to Princess Danae. They split, giving them space to walk forward.

They wind their way through the city, passing a butcher hanging a fresh pig up to cure, a blacksmith hammering at a large axe, and a few children running after a rooster.

Elis tugs on Emit's sleeve when he turns to watch the rooster race by. "Eyes ahead."

"Sorry," Emit whispers. "But did you see the size of that thing!"

"Stay close as we enter the market," Princess Danae says, looking over her shoulder.

The murmur of the crowd grows as the path narrows. The tables that line the smooth stone alley are piled high with various wares, including colorful pottery, fruits, vegetables, breads, and tethered live chickens and ducks.

They pass a group of teen boys. One mocks a bow to Princess Danae before another throws a tomato. It splatters on the back of Elis's red shirt. He cuts a look back and fakes drawing a sword from his waist.

The boys scatter.

Elis doesn't lose step with Emit. "Ignorance is not a trait we invented," he whispers to Emit.

Emit glares up at Elis. "Who is we?"

"Kids our age," Elis says, smiling. "Not *us*."

Emit nods.

"Through here," Princess Danae says, pointing to an archway.

Ora spots the sundial. She runs ahead of Zana and the others.

"Ora!" Zana yells. "Wait!"

The crowd swarms around Ora. She's consumed by the people, carts and animals. She loses sight of the sundial and tries to fight her way back.

"Ora!" Emit yells, jumping up and down. "Come back!"

"Emit stay with Zana," Elis says, "I'll get Ora."

Princess Danae takes Zana's hand and reaches for Emit's hand. "It's important we stay together."

Emit folds his arms across his chest and pouts.

"Please," Elis says, "just stay put."

"Find Ora!" Emit says.

"I will!" Elis says.

"You lost Ora?" Danae asks.

The replay pauses on Elis shoving past a group of people.

"Just wait," Elis says, holding up a hand.

The replay continues.

Elis weaves his way around a large cart carrying animal hides and spots Ora ahead of the next cluster of people.

"Ora!" Elis shouts.

Ora turns but is shoved forward by a familiar dark-haired woman.

"Andromeda!" Elis shouts.

140

"Stop," Ora says to her, "I need to go back!"

Andromeda shakes her head and grips Ora's arm. "You should have never come here!" She yanks Ora into a small alley and shoves her through an open doorway. She slams the door closed behind them.

"Let go!" Ora yells. "Elis, I'm in here!"

Andromeda covers Ora's mouth. "Be quiet!"

Ora bites Andromeda's hand.

"Ouch!"

Ora kicks her in the shins and fumbles with the door.

"You fool!" Andromeda steps between Ora and the door. "It's too late."

"Elis!" Ora cries out.

"Perendi was right behind Elis," Andromeda says, shoving Ora away from the door. "If you don't keep your mouth shut. You could be next!"

Ora whimpers. "I need to warn him."

"You need to remain quiet," Andromeda says.

⚡

"Ora!" Elis shouts as thunder claps overhead. He turns, Princess Danae waves him back. Elis shakes his head, but she points above him. He glances up at the darkening sky. Lightning streaks down and strikes the ground between him and Princess Danae.

The ground ripples and throws Elis back. A cloud of smoke and dirt blocks his view as he crashes into the stunned crowd.

"Elis!" Zana shouts. She pulls against Princess Danae's grip. "Let go! He could be hurt."

Emit points to the ground. "It's opening!"

The crack in the ground widens and races towards the sundial.

Elis stands brushing off the dirt. He lifts his shirt to wipe his eyes, but his vision is still blurred by the smoke rising from a burning cart of straw blocking his route back to the courtyard.

A shadow falls over Elis. He glances up and finds Hermes hovering just over his head.

"Time to go, kid," Hermes says, extending his hand to Elis.

"But Ora," Elis says.

"I'll come back," Hermes says. "I promise."

Elis looks back one more time but can't find Ora's brown curls in the crowd. He takes Hermes's hand, and they are airborne.

Elis closes his eyes as they fly through the smoke. He hears Zana cry out and his eyes fly open.

Princess Danae is holding Zana back.

Hermes lowers Elis to the ground. "Get the hourglass and stay out of sight." He points to the splitting stones holding the sundial. "I'll get Ora."

Zana wrenches her arm free and launches herself into Elis's arms. "Are you ok?"

"Yes," Elis says, squeezing her in a tight hug.

"Did you see Ora?" Emit asks, his voice shaky and face stained with tears.

"Andromeda took her down an alley just before the lightning struck," Elis says, sitting Zana down. "Perendi is close. We need to get the hourglass out of here and quick."

Princess Danae nods. "There is a safe passage through there." She points to a stone wall.

Elis frowns.

"It's a hidden door that leads down to a cave near the ember archway and Pemphredo's home."

Elis shakes his head. "We aren't leaving until we get Ora back."

The ground shakes and the stones around the sundial crumbles.

"Elis," Princess Danae says. "We are out of time. Get the hourglass."

Zana tugs Elis's hand. "Hermes will find Ora."

Emit edges closer to the sundial. "I can see it!" He reaches for the hourglass. "I can get it."

"No, wait!" Elis says, stepping between Emit and the sundial.

Elis leans over the sundial and spots the gilded cage around the hourglass. He reaches over the edge of the remaining stones.

The ground shakes again and the hourglass shifts further down.

"Elis," Princess Danae says. "Grab it before it falls any further."

Elis grasps the hourglass, but his hands are trembling. He fumbles his grip, and it slips, tipping to one side.

"No!" Elis says, catching it with a fingertip. He gently pulls it up and grasps it with two hands. He examines the sand inside. It's evenly split between the sides. "Now what?"

Thunder rattles the ground.

Princess Danae looks up. "We need to go, now!" She bustles Zana and Emit towards the stone wall.

Elis carefully follows, attempting to keep every grain of sand on either side from shifting through the gap between.

The princess bends at the base of the wall and brushes some dirt away until her fingers find metal. She fingers the loop and pulls up. The stones hiss as a section of the wall opens inward.

"The steps are steep," Princess Danae says. "Be careful."

Elis looks for Hermes or Ora. "Come on, Hermy." He carefully steps into the opening.

Princess Danae releases the loop and darts in behind Elis before the door closes.

"It's really dark," Zana says, shivering.

Princess Danae reaches inside her gown and pulls out a light stone. She taps it and tosses it up.

The stone spins and adjusts from bright white to a soft glow illuminating the steep stone stairwell.

Emit teeters on the landing. "Whoa."

"Just go slowly," Princess Danae says. She hikes up her tunic and steps down at an angle. She makes it down about ten steps. "Alright Emit come on down."

Emit takes a step down and hastily turns to face backwards. "I think we should climb down—like it's a ladder."

Elis peeks over the edge. "Good idea, but still go slowly."

Emit nods.

Zana hangs back. "How are you going to carry that down?"

"Super, super slowly." Elis winks. "Go on, just take one step at a time."

Zana follows Emit's approach.

"That's great," Elis says. He waits for Zana to clear about ten steps before testing his balance on the first step. He turns at an angle and gradually shifts his weight while keeping the hourglass level. *One step at a time.*

32

Hermes glides over the crowd, split by the crevice that grows wider as the ground rattles and buildings shift on their cracking foundations.

"Where is little Ora?"

He spots a familiar red hood at the far end of the market. He glides over and sees Pemphredo disarming a man.

Hermes lands a hard kick to the side of the man's head.

"I had him," Pemphredo says, glaring at Hermes.

"You're welcome," Hermes says. "Why are you back in the city?"

"To find this." Pemphredo holds up a tiny scale.

"Did you lift that from the apothecary?"

"Maybe," Pemphredo says, tucking the scale back in the bag slung over her shoulder.

"Andromeda has Ora," Hermes says.

"No!" Pemphredo back hands Hermes shoulder. "How in the hell did that happen?"

"Forget how," Hermes says. "Where would she hide a little girl?"

"Where did she take her from?" Pemphredo asks, taking his hand as they push off.

He flies them over to the courtyard with the broken sundial and drops them down. "She got shoved by the crowd in this direction."

"What happened here?" Pemphredo asks, pointing to the giant crevice.

"Perendi."

"Did they get the hourglass out?" Pemphredo asks, inspecting the sundial.

"Yes," Hermes says, nodding to the stone wall. "They're heading to your home now."

"They left without Ora?"

"I promised to find her," Hermes says. "So, help me. Where would Andromeda hide Ora?"

"There's a passage to the grottos beneath a shop down that way," Pemphredo says, pointing in the direction Ora had been going. "Start there. And have Zeus summon Andromeda to his quarters. She can't ignore him."

"You're not coming?" Hermes asks. "I thought you were sworn to protect time!"

"Half of time plus the compass are headed in that direction." Pemphredo points towards her home. "I can't reach my sisters, and you have speed over this mess." She gestures to the ground. "I need to go." She pats the bag. "They'll need the scale."

Hermes glances at the crowd gathering around them jeering for answers. "Go."

Pemphredo runs for the stone wall across from the sundial.

Hermes flies up and over the crowd.

A large shadow falls over the courtyard.

Pemphredo feels the hair on her neck stand a second before the lightning strikes.

Stones fly and the ground sinks into a gaping hole.

Pemphredo free falls along with a dozen others. Her bag snags on an exposed root. She dangles head down, watching the screaming men and women continue to fall. She feels a hand grip her ankle.

"Hold on!" Hermes says, holding Pemphredo and attempting to release her bag.

The root cracks.

"It's going to break!" Pemphredo twists and thrusts her hand into the bag. She grabs the scale. "Fly!"

Hermes pulls and Pemphredo lets the bag fall over her head. She manages to hold on to the scale as they fly up over the city. Hermes drifts over to Pemphredo's stone cottage.

"How far did you get before you saw me fall?" Pemphredo asks, straightening her tunic as they land near the cottage.

"Not far," Hermes says, panting. He shakes his head. "There were so many people."

"I know," Pemphredo whispers.

"Hermes!"

Pemphredo turns. "Was that one of the kids?"

Hermes flies straight up and spots Emit running up the hill from the cave. "Are you alone?"

"Princess Danae fell!" Emit says, squinting at Hermes. "Where is Ora?"

Hermes flies towards Emit. "I am still looking for Ora. Is the princess hurt?"

Emit points to the cave. "We can't see her."

"Pemphredo is just up the hill at the cottage," Hermes says. "I'll send Zana and Elis up there. Go inside and stay away from the windows."

"But Ora," Emit says.

"I'll find her!" Hermes gestures towards the cottage. "Go!"

Emit huffs but turns and walks up the hill. Hermes flies down to the cave.

Elis and Zana are standing with their backs to Hermes when he lands.

"What happened?" Hermes asks.

Zana jumps.

"Careful," Hermes says, pulling Zana away from the edge.

Elis wobbles with the hourglass.

"Why did you sneak up on us like that?" Zana asks, wiggling out of his grasp.

"Emit said the princess fell," Hermes says.

Elis nods. "The ground shook so hard—and she just fell."

"Down there?" Hermes steps closer to the edge. "I don't see her—or the bottom."

Elis leans close to Hermes and whispers, "I never heard her land."

"Pemphredo and Emit are up at the cottage. Go up and stay inside."

Elis hesitates.

"What is it?" Hermes asks.

"Ora."

"She'll be ok," Hermes says.

Elis frowns. "If anything..."

"Elis, I will find her."

Elis nods then turns to Zana. "Come on."

Hermes waits until their backs are to him. Then he dives off the edge and flies straight down. *Please don't be dead.*

33

Itra leans forward. "Can we hit pause?"

Elis nods, and the image of Hermes's drawn face freezes.

"Do you want to tell us now or wait for us to see it?" Itra asks.

Elis shakes his head. "What do you mean?"

"I don't think we need to witness her crumpled body." Itra looks over at Danae. She shakes her head.

"We assure you she's fine," Zana says, leaning forward with her palms turned up on the table. "Trust us. We need you to see everything, to help you understand."

"Zana," Kaly says. "Don't you just want to tell us?"

"No mom." Zana takes her hand. "Trust us."

Leon drums the table. "You heard her. Let it roll."

Hermes's hair billows back. He tucks into a somersault and rolls to a stop in the air. He drops his toes down to test the surface. They dip into something wet. He flies up higher and strains to see what's below him. He pats down his tunic until he finds a light stone. He frantically grabs it, taps it, and tosses it up.

Light fills the cavern.

Hermes inspects his reflection on the water below. He quickly dives in and pries his eyes open. He spots a piece of fabric further down and kicks harder to investigate.

The light follows him below the surface.

Hermes sees Princess Danae struggling. He pulls on her hands. She shakes her head and points to her ankle. Her foot is stuck under a rock.

Hermes fights the fire exploding through his chest and shimmies the rock until her foot is freed. The princess goes limp.

Hermes plants his feet on the rock and wraps his arms around Princess Danae's waist. He pushes off.

They shoot out of the water at torpedo speed. He exhales as they land on the ledge inside the cave. He rolls the princess to her side. She coughs up heaps of water and gasps for air.

"You're fine," Hermes says, patting her back. "But your ankle may be broken."

She rolls to her back and pants. "The children?"

"All but Ora are up the hill with Pemphredo."

She attempts to sit up but falls back. "Ora," she says. "What happened?"

Hermes shakes his head. "All hell broke loose. The sundial and courtyard are gone. A huge sink hole swallowed everything after another strike from Perendi."

"How many?" She closes her eyes and her bottom lip quivers.

"A few dozen," Hermes says, sitting back and wrapping his hands around his knees. "I grabbed Pemphredo, but I didn't have time to rescue anyone else."

Princess Danae pounds the ground with her fists. "It's all so messed up."

"Let's get you up the hill and into some dry clothes."

"I'll manage on my own," she says. "Get Ora!"

Hermes stands and offers his hand.

Princess Danae takes his hand and lets him help her up. She tests her weight on her injured ankle and winces but nods. "Thanks, now go!"

Hermes bows and steps outside the cave. He looks back. Princess Danae waves him away. Hermes pushes off and flies back towards the city. He soars up over the stone buildings until he reaches a balcony. He lands and kicks the door open to the suite of Andromeda and Perseus.

"Andromeda!" Hermes shouts, opening the wardrobe and checking under the large bed.

"Why are you shouting?" Zeus asks, pushing open the door to the suite from the corridor.

"Andromeda took a little girl, and Perendi has killed several dozen people," Hermes says, pointing at Zeus. "And he nearly killed your wife."

"Danae!" Zeus stammers.

"She's safe," Hermes says. "No, thanks to you, dad. Where the hell have you been?"

"Inspecting the sunken courtyard," Zeus says. "My men are searching for Perendi and his followers now."

"Have you seen Andromeda?" Hermes asks, pushing past Zeus to the adjacent living room.

"Not for two or three days."

"Summon her back to the castle at once."

Zeus folds his arms across his massive chest. "Why?"

"Were you not listening?" Hermes asks, checking behind the curtains. "She's taken a little girl named Ora."

Zeus lifts a single eyebrow.

"As in Ember's *time*," Hermes says. "Emit and Ora."

Zeus's eyes go wide. "Andromeda would never… Perseus would kill her!"

"It was Perseus that dragged her into this mess to begin with!"

"Where is he?" Zeus asks.

"Trapped, thanks to Ember," Hermes says. "Are you going to summon her back or not?"

"Of course," Zeus says. "Andromeda, I summon you to my chambers."

"Elis?" Princess Danae says, pushing open the door to the cottage.

"You're alive!" Emit says, running towards her. He crashes into her, wrapping his arms around her waist. "But wet! Ew."

"That's what happens when you fall into water," she says, laughing. She glances around the room and spots the hourglass. "Any issues?"

"No," Elis says.

"I have a fresh tunic," Pemphredo says, waving her to one of the four doors. "Kids, stay away from the windows and do not venture outside."

Elis and Zana nod.

"You're limping," Emit says, watching the princess walk.

She winks at Emit. "It's nothing to worry about."

Emit frowns. "Elis, do you think they have ice?"

Elis laughs. "Not likely."

"But mom always puts ice on my sore spots."

"Look around Emit," Elis says, extending his arms. "Do you see any plugs or wires for electricity?"

The bare stone walls rise to a height just over Elis. The wooden beams overhead are covered with a thatched roof.

"Electricity hasn't been invented yet," Zana says. "I think it's wonderful!"

"Do you think this works?" Emit asks, holding up his wrist with the gold bracelet.

"What works?" Pemphredo asks, emerging with a nearly dry princess.

"Ora and I can communicate," Emit says, tapping a solid piece of gold. "Ora, can you hear me?"

152

"Emit!" Ora shouts.

"Where are you?" Emit asks.

"In a dark room," Ora says. "Andromeda made me go down like a thousand steps. She screamed something about Zeus before yelling at me to stay put and locked me inside this room."

Emit looks up at Princess Danae as she rushes to his side. "Zeus is your husband?"

The princess nods. "Hermes has sent word to Zeus to summon her to the castle." She steps closer and kneels to Emit's level. "Can she hear me?"

"Ora?" Emit asks. "Can you hear the princess?"

"Yes," Ora says.

"Did you see any markings on the steps or in the corridor?" Princess Danae asks. "Or on the door?"

"It was all very dark," Ora says, "but I can feel a mark on the back of the door."

"Can you describe it?" Emit asks.

"A wing, maybe."

Pemphredo and Princess Danae glance at each other. They shrug.

"Anything else?" Emit asks.

"I found another wing," Ora says.

"Like a bird or a butterfly?" Emit asks.

"Bird," Ora says. "A big bird!"

Pemphredo claps. "The usmu."

"Perendi's war room?" Princess Danae asks, standing.

"Possibly," Pemphredo says.

"Is that close?" Elis asks.

"No," the princess says. "It's on the far side of the city."

"I think I hear footsteps overhead," Ora says.

"We're coming," Emit says, "hide until you hear our special knock."

Emit taps the bracelet and Ora falls silent.

"How do these bracelets work?" Pemphredo asks.

"I don't know," Emit says. "All I know is it allows us to speak to other wearers."

"Who else has one?" Pemphredo asks.

Elis and Zana push back their sleeves and hold up their wrists.

"Plus, our parents," Emit says. "And Anton."

"Do they work across dimensions?" Pemphredo asks.

Emit shrugs. "Ora and I found out by accident. We never asked how it worked."

"Can you try your parents?" Princess Danae asks.

Emit nods. He presses the solid gold link. "Mom! Dad!"

Emit's young voice echoes around the dining hall. "Mom! Dad! Mom! Dad!"

"What the devil is that?" Danae asks, looking at Emit.

"Our calling card coming through a little later than we planned," Emit says.

"It's been about an hour since you were sent to the archives," Leon says, checking his watch. "The playback has been rolling for forty-five minutes or so."

"So did time reverse?" Danae asks.

"It's called a time echo," Elis says.

"Explain," Leon says.

"The parallel dimensions didn't experience the rapid time change imprinted here. Essentially, it's a sound reverberation of your real-time events here. Our bracelets work across dimensions but not across rapidly changing time."

Danae fidgets with the bracelet. "We thought you were just down in the archives."

"Is Chronos still here?" Itra asks.

"*Junior,*" Leon says.

154

"I just caught my reflection in the window," Junior says, wheezing. *"Is it just me or did I age about forty years?"*

"Thirty," Leon says. *"What's happening in the maze?"*

"Nothing," Junior says. *"The ghost-like appearance of Chronos is frozen with one arm raised to his shoulder palm out and the other pointing at the fairy statue."*

Leon shakes his head and relays the message to the others. "Apparently Chronos, or whatever he is here, is frozen."

"Frozen?" Kaly asks.

"Junior said he has one arm raised like this." Leon raises his hand palm out and points across the table with his other hand. "And he is pointing at the fairy statue."

Elis shifts in his chair.

"Elis," Itra says. "Do you know what this means?"

Elis glances at Zana. She nods.

"He's swearing to exchange Ora for his freedom," Elis says.

Danae slaps the table. "She's been captured for thirty years?"

Zana sighs. "It's complicated."

"Mom," Emit says. "We're trying to show you—everything."

Itra turns, blocking Danae from Emit. He levels his nose with Emit. "Son, is your sister alive and well?"

"Yes."

Itra nods. "Ok, let's continue." He glances at Danae's tear-streaked cheeks. "If you're ok?"

Danae takes in a long breath. "I'm ok."

"Why aren't they answering?" Emit asks.

"Dad," Elis says, pressing the link on his bracelet.

"Elis!" Anton answers. "Where are you? I don't recognize the room you're in."

Elis looks around the room. "How are you seeing us?"

"The pocket watch."

"We are in the City of Time with Pemphredo and Princess Danae," Elis says. "Are you still in the castle?"

"No," Anton says. "I'm at home in the apartment. Wait a minute. I don't see Ora with you."

Elis hesitates and looks at Emit.

Emit shrugs. "Truth?"

"Elis," Anton says. "Are you there?"

"Zana and Emit are with me and we recovered the hourglass."

"Is Ora back at the castle?" Anton asks.

"No," Elis says. "She's here in the City of Time."

"Elis," Anton says.

"We were separated," Elis says. "But please don't worry. We'll find her."

"Let me check on her," Anton says. "Show me Ora. Elis, she's in a dark room. I can't see anything helpful."

"Can you talk to Itra or Danae?" Elis asks.

"They're not answering," Anton says.

"Zana will try Kaly and Leon."

Emit shows Zana where to press down on her bracelet. "Mom? Dad?"

Zana presses down again. "Kaly! Leon!" She stomps her foot. "Why can't they hear us?"

Pemphredo and Princess Danae exchange worried glances.

"Dad," Elis says. "They're not answering us either."

"I'll get in the car and head towards the Castle of Teskom," Anton says. "Find Ora."

"Yes, sir."

34

"Zeus," Andromeda says, marching down the corridor. "I'm here, my lord!"

"And where is your husband?" Zeus asks, filling the door to his chambers.

Andromeda halts. "Um. He's a little busy at the moment."

Zeus folds his arms over his chest and raises a single eyebrow.

"Um," Andromeda whispers.

"Where is the girl?"

Andromeda's mouth falls open. "How..." She feels a tap on her shoulder and slowly looks behind her.

Hermes smiles and pinches his nose. "You smell like burnt hair!"

Andromeda lifts a finger with purpose and scowls when he remains standing.

Hermes laughs. "What, did you forget?" He circles around her to stand next to Zeus. "Your jewelry was melted into ash along with your hair."

"Speaking of," Andromeda says, "has Zeus decided how he will punish you?"

"Ha!" Zeus marches forward and stands an inch from her. "You trespassed inside the Castle of Teskom, kidnapped four children, assaulted my son, and then kidnapped one of the four a second time."

Andromeda bows. "It was all a giant misunderstanding."

"You can explain that misunderstanding after you take me to the girl."

"But Peren—"

"Don't you dare finish his name in my presence!" He points down the corridor. "Walk. Now. Silently!"

Andromeda turns, straightens her spine, throws back her shoulders and lifts her chin.

"Check on my wife," Zeus says to Hermes.

Hermes nods and bows at the waist. "Meet you at Pemphredo's?"

"Yes," Zeus says, following Andromeda down the corridor.

Hermes lands and knocks on the wooden door.

Pemphredo pulls it open. "Where's Ora?"

"Andromeda is taking Zeus to her as we speak," Hermes says, ducking to enter the cottage. "He asked me to check on Princess Danae." He looks around the vacant room.

"Where is she?" Hermes asks. A wall six inches from him fades and reveals the princess and the children.

"Sorry," Princess Danae says. "We are still on high alert."

Hermes nods. "Smart move."

"We think we know where she is," Princess Danae says. "Emit can talk to her."

"How?"

Emit holds up his wrist with the gold bracelet. "Ora, Hermes is here."

"Hi Hermes," Ora says.

Hermes whirls around looking for her.

Elis smirks. "Pretty cool, right?"

"Ora, a man named Zeus will be there soon with Andromeda."

"I hope he gets here soon," Ora says. "There's shouting overhead. I heard them say something about the hourglass."

Pemphredo peeks out the window. "Perendi's likely giving his men marching orders to find us. This will be the first place they look."

Princess Danae corners Hermes. "Where are you meeting Zeus?"

"Here."

She grabs his thumb with the gold ring. "Open a portal door to the archives."

"I'll try." Hermes steps back. "Protect time, unite to fight. Ember of mine."

A door appears but flickers.

"Ugh!" Hermes shakes out his hand.

Zana steps beside him. "Take my hand. We'll say it together."

Hermes grasps her tiny hand and nods.

They chant in unison, "Protect time, unite to fight. Ember of mine."

A door appears but remains closed.

Zana presses the handle, but it's locked.

"I see at least five men climbing the hill." Pemphredo motions with her hands to move away from the door. "Try somewhere here in the City of Time."

"My quarters," Princess Danae says.

Hermes nods and the door flies open to familiar stone walls and purple drapes fixed to either side of the entrance to a large balcony.

"Elis, carefully pick up the hourglass," Pemphredo says, ushering Zana and Emit inside the open door. "Hermes, whatever you do to distract them—just don't burn the place down."

Princess Danae follows Elis inside the door, but she hesitates. "Go to Perendi's war room. Catch up with Zeus."

Hermes nods and bows.

Hermes checks the window and spots two of the five men. He steps out of the cottage and leaves the door wide open. "Come back!" He watches the two men slow and lower their stance. "Wait!" He shouts and starts to run away from the approaching men.

They charge towards him, bypassing the house.

Hermes launches into the sky and circles the men.

One man notches an arrow.

"What are you waiting for?" Hermes says, pointing towards the city. "They're getting away with the hourglass."

The other men hustle past the archer, bumping his arm. He releases the arrow. It goes wide—missing Hermes.

Hermes flies towards the city. He spots one man ducking into the open cottage. He emerges, shaking his head.

"Whew," Hermes mutters, dodging a tall evergreen. He hangs back under the cover of the trees and watches.

The armed men take the worn, tree-lined path.

He spots the last of the men catching up with the others and flies higher. He scans the sky; the light is falling to dusk. "Come on Zeus!"

"Keep walking," Zeus says, pushing Andromeda forward.

"Shoving me is not necessary," Andromeda says, lengthening her stride. "She's safe."

160

"Anywhere here is not safe," Zeus says. "Perendi will do anything to find favor with Chronos and you, my dear traitor, should know all about that."

"I'm not..." Andromeda pauses at a splintered door. "Oh, no."

"Andromeda," Zeus says, pushing past her. He removes the remaining door. "It's empty. Where is she?"

Andromeda cowers and backs against the wall.

Zeus steps close to her. "Your idea of safe was leaving a child in the war room of the very man who seeks her?"

"I, uh, um," Andromeda whispers. "I'm sorry. You summoned me and I had no choice."

"You're a fool," Zeus says, "to assign blame to me." He pulls back his arm in a wide arc and a thunderbolt appears. He angles the bolt to Andromeda's chest. "Give me one reason to spare your life, you sorry excuse for a daughter-in-law."

"Chronos wants Ember back by his side," Andromeda says. "And he will use the girl to bargain for her hand."

"Ember is not a fool," Zeus says, inching the static tip closer to her chest.

"Ora is time," Andromeda says, wincing as the heat of his weapon wafts over her chest. "She can slow time to a stop."

"And this is relevant?"

"She can stop time in every dimension but the past."

"Not new news." Zeus raises the thunderbolt.

"Wait!" Andromeda cries. "I'm pregnant."

Zeus narrows his eyes. "You're lying."

Andromeda shakes her head and lets her tears fall. "I've missed two cycles."

Zeus takes a small step back. "If you've dared to lie, your punishment will be worse than the rock you were once tied to."

Andromeda swallows a sob. "I swear by your wife's name—I am with child."

Zeus snarls, baring his teeth. "By my wife's name." He spits at her feet.

Andromeda grimaces. "Are you done?"

"Done?" Zeus takes another step back.

"We need to find Ora," Andromeda says, looking down the corridor. "And judging by the path of destruction, I would say we follow her that way."

Andromeda points. Zeus glances down the corridor—remnants of splintered wood, a few askew paintings, and shattered pieces of pottery are scattered on the ground near the far exit.

"Where were you held by Chronos?" Zeus asks.

"In the grottos near the ley lines."

35

Danae pushes back from the table. "This is too much!"

"Mom," Emit says, going to her side. "We need to show you what happens."

"Emit," Danae says, cupping his chin. "My dear beautiful boy. There is only so much drama I can take in one sitting."

Emit frowns. "Now wait a minute. You can watch The Notebook or Steel Magnolia over and over, knowing that you will end up in a puddle of tears at the end. That's a drama with trauma."

Itra laughs.

Danae glares in his direction.

"He's got a point," Itra says.

"Hang in there," Emit says, hugging Danae. "We are almost to the kicking ass and taking names part of the adventure."

Danae squeezes him. "I hope so."

Emit plops down in his chair.

"Are you ready?" Elis asks, leaning forward and extending a hand to Danae.

Danae scoots her chair back up to the table. "Bring it on." She reaches across the table, taking Elis's hand, and she nods to Kaly and Leon.

They nod with a firm smile.

"Let's roll," Zana says.

Hermes flies to a turret overlooking the city center and lands. He looks down at the dark gaping pit and the abandoned market.

Where are the people?

He scans the horizon as a low rumble of thunder starts from the north. The hairs on his neck stand instantly. He looks back towards the tree line and spots Perendi's men starting their descent towards the city walls.

Zeus, where are you?

Hermes pushes off and flies for Princess Danae's quarters. He pauses when people emerge from a pub below. He watches the crowd gather and a few men are shouting orders.

What did they say?

Hermes flies low enough to hear the murmur of the crowd.

"Find Pemphredo," a man says to a group of teens. They are armed with slingshots and pouches of rocks. A few have daggers strapped to their thighs, and one kid has a bow and three arrows.

"Find the witch!" a woman cries. "Make Pemphredo pay for what she's done!"

Hermes perches on a roof ledge. "Why are you blaming Pemphredo?"

The crowd turns their attention towards him. A few men draw their swords.

A woman points up at Hermes. "She opened the pit of despair and took my baby away."

Hermes shakes his head. "She would never. The pit was created by Perendi in his search for something that doesn't belong to him." He points up to the darkening sky. "If you want to persecute somebody—it's Perendi and his goons."

The crowd jeers.

"Zeus and Princess Danae will reward anyone who captures Perendi and his men," Hermes announces.

"What kind of reward?" a man asks, stepping out of the shadows and exposing his long white beard.

164

Chronos? Hermes squints. Then he says, "The reward will be life-changing wealth."

The crowd scatters with a collective whoop.

Hermes doesn't blink, fixated on the man.

He comes closer. The flicker of a lit torch illuminates the features of his face.

Hermes gasps. "Chronos!"

The man grins and nods his head. "At your service."

Hermes blinks and Chronos vanishes. "He's gone." Hermes searches the remaining men and women loitering about. "The kids." He pushes off and flies towards Danae's quarters.

The clouds erupt in a chorus of thunder.

Hermes dodges a lightning bolt. He looks over his shoulder and spots Perendi punching a fist into his palm.

BOOM

Hermes covers his ears and free falls. He recovers only inches from a pointed turret. He whirls around, searching the clouds.

Where is Zeus?

Hermes looks up towards the castle—a light flashes inside. "No, no, no!" He aims his flight to the balcony just outside of Danae's suite.

"Emit!" Princess Danae shouts. "Stay here."

"But Ora!" Emit cries, jiggling the handle to the door. "She needs me!"

Elis kneels next to Emit. "Hey, just take a breath. Let's try to call her again."

Emit sniffles and taps his bracelet. "Ora, can you hear me?"

Tap, tap

"What was that?" Zana asks.

Pemphredo turns to the window. "It's Hermes!"

Princess Danae and Pemphredo hastily open the window.

"Hermes," Pemphredo says, hauling him in.

"There's trouble inside," Hermes says breathlessly, pointing to the door. "Perendi's here in the castle." He holds up his thumb. "Where to now?"

"But Ora!" Emit cries again. Elis wraps Emit in a hug.

Emit resists and pounds his fists against Elis's chest.

"Have you heard from her?" Hermes asks.

Zana nods.

"She thought it was Zeus coming to get her," Zana says. "But it was a man with a long white beard." She frowns. "He took her, and she hasn't answered us since."

"Where is Zeus?" Pemphredo asks.

Hermes shrugs. "I haven't seen him, but I swear I saw a man in the city that looks like Chronos." He gestures pulling a beard from his chin. "I blinked and he was gone."

A howl of air rattles the suite's door.

"Time's up, we need to go," Hermes says. "Protect time, unite to fight. Ember of mine."

A door opens to a sandy floor.

"Where is this?" Pemphredo asks, hesitantly looking in.

"The revolutionary dimension," Hermes says.

Princess Danae shakes her head. "We don't have cloaks."

The suite's door hinges groan under pressure.

Hermes slams the portal door shut. "Where can we go?"

"Try the archives again?" Pemphredo suggests.

"Protect time, unite to fight. Ember of mine." Hermes reaches for the new door, but it flickers.

The door to the suite cracks.

Hermes stomps his foot. "Ember, a little help here!"

A door shimmers into existence and opens.

"Go!" Hermes says.

Princess Danae takes Zana's hand. "Come on." They step through.

166

"I know you're in there!" Perendi shouts, banging on the suite's door.

"Elis, take the hourglass," Pemphredo says. She hands the scale to Emit. "Take this and go. We'll be right behind you with Ora."

The door shimmers and starts to flicker.

"Hurry Elis," Hermes says, holding the door open for him.

Elis delicately balances the hourglass and steps through behind Emit.

The door vanishes.

Pemphredo turns to Hermes. "I hope you can get us back to them!"

Hermes grabs Pemphredo's hand and yanks her away from the suite's door.

The door explodes with a giant bolt of lightning.

Hermes shields her from flying shards of wood and pushes her towards the open window.

Pemphredo climbs out on the ledge.

Hermes wraps his arms around her middle and flies out.

"Oof," Pemphredo exhales, watching the flames shoot out of the windows and balcony door.

"That was close," Hermes says, flying them up and over the castle.

"Too close," Pemphredo says. "We need Zeus."

Hermes circles. "I'm pretty sure Zeus is answering the call." He points down to a clash of lightning bursting out of the castle.

"Where the hell is Ora?" Pemphredo asks, craning her neck. "How well do you know the grottos?"

"I used to play hide and seek with a few kids down there," Hermes says, "when I was six."

"It's more than the one and only time I've been down there." She gestures to a stone wall at the farthest perimeter of the city. "Take us down near the north entrance."

Hermes dips and weaves through the stone structures until he glides them to a stop.

Pemphredo pushes her windswept hair down and ties it back with a strap of leather from around her wrist. After her low ponytail is secure, she marches towards a darkened stairwell.

"Well, don't just stand there," Pemphredo says, looking over her shoulder.

"Sorry," Hermes says, adjusting the length of his tunic. "I can't really fly down there."

Pemphredo rolls her eyes. "If we miss Ora, I'll let you explain to her mother why we were late." She darts inside and down a stairwell.

Hermes follows close behind.

They stop as they near the ground.

"Do you hear whimpering?" Pemphredo whispers.

"Yes!" Hermes charges forward, but Pemphredo snags his arm dragging him up a step.

"Don't be stupid," Pemphredo says. "If it's truly Chronos, I need to go in first. I can counter any attempt he makes to slow our progress."

Hermes frowns, but nods.

They slowly descend the last few steps. The entry widens to a smooth cavern with four large marble statues anchoring the rounded space giving it symmetry. An eternal fire basin in the center highlights the sand and shells covering the ground.

Pemphredo points to a set of large footprints heading in their direction.

"He must have gone out the way we came in," Hermes says, looking over his shoulder. The darkened stairwell stares back. He shivers.

"Focus," Pemphredo whispers.

Hermes grasps the hilt of his dagger. He follows Pemphredo. They stay close to the cavern walls.

"Emit, can you hear me?" Ora says.

Pemphredo and Hermes race towards her voice.

Ora whimpers and sniffles.

"Ora," Pemphredo whispers.

"Over here!" Ora says.

Pemphredo's eyes land on a large Pegasus statue. A little hand waves from between the wings and the horse's head. "Ora, it's Pemphredo and Hermes."

"Help me," Ora says.

"How did you end up here?" Hermes says, climbing up the side of the horse.

"A man took me from the dark room," Ora says, holding up her mangled bracelet. "He broke it!"

Hermes frowns. "Are you hurt?"

She shakes her head. "Just scared."

"Come on down," Hermes says. He reaches for Ora and she slides down off the back of the horse. He catches her and hops down from the statue. "Protect time, unite to fight. Ember of mine."

A door appears between Hermes and Pemphredo.

Pemphredo opens the door. "Where does this go?"

"Hopefully to the others," Hermes says, handing off Ora to Pemphredo.

"You're not coming?" Pemphredo asks, stepping through the door.

"I'm going to try to make sure Perendi and Zeus don't destroy the city."

Pemphredo nods.

"Be careful Hermy," Ora says.

Hermes smiles and bows his head to Ora. "I promise I'll try." He winks and pulls the door shut. It vanishes.

36

"Ora!" Emit shouts, running towards Ora and Pemphredo.

Ora scrambles down from Pemphredo and runs towards Emit. They crash into each other and roll to the ground entangled in a hug.

Zana leaps onto the pile and hugs Ora.

"Can't breathe," Ora wheezes.

"Ok," Elis says. "Let her up for a breath. Are you ok, Miss Ora?"

She stands with the help of Zana and Emit. "Yes."

Zana gasps and points to Ora's hair.

"What is it?" Ora asks, patting her head.

"Your hair," Zana says, taking a strand and pulling it in front of Ora's face. "It's white."

Ora jerks back.

Zana accidentally pulls the hair.

"Ouch," Ora says, rubbing her scalp.

"Sorry," Zana says. "It's like Aunt Pem's hair but all over."

Princess Danae leans forward to inspect her hair. "It's pure white, not a single dark strand left." She kneels to Ora's level. "I think it suits you. It's really pretty." She pats her shoulder and stands. "And it might be temporary."

Elis nods. "According to my science teacher, hair evolves over a lifetime—changing textures and colors."

Ora pulls her hair forward. "Mom's going to freak out!"

Emit laughs. "True, so true."

Princess Danae steps beside Pemphredo.

"I didn't notice her hair until we stepped through," Pemphredo whispers.

"Where was she?" the princess asks.

"In the grottos sitting astride the Pegasus statue."

Princess Danae turns her back to the kids to shield her frown. "Why would he just leave her there? Was she alone?"

Pemphredo nods. "We saw a set of footprints leading towards the north stairwell, but other than that, there way no evidence of anyone else in the space."

"The north stairwell is closest to the lake..." She looks over her shoulder eying Ora thoughtfully. She turns back to Pemphredo. "What happened after we left?"

"Zeus found Perendi in the castle." Pemphredo smirks. "I'm pretty sure you will be in need of some new linens upon your return."

The princess sighs. "If we can return."

"What do you mean?" Pemphredo asks.

"Look around," the princess says.

Pemphredo scans the room for the first time. The circular space is draped in dusty purple silks. The light hovering above appears to be a light stone. She spots a small bed shoved in the corner and a table buried in a layer of dust. A few broken chairs are scattered about the space and a single frame hangs on the wall.

"Where are we?" Pemphredo asks.

"My original hell," the princess says.

"No!" Pemphredo whispers. "It can't be!"

The princess nods. "This is where my father imprisoned me until I gave birth to Perseus."

"How could Hermes do this?" Pemphredo asks, shaking her head.

"I don't think he did," the princess says, nudging her away from the children.

"But..." Pemphredo says.

The princess holds up her hand. "He asked for Ember's help right before the door became solid."

"Why would she choose this hole?" Pemphredo asks.

"Maybe because the only person who should be able to find us is Zeus."

"Blocking Chronos and Perendi." Pemphredo exhales. "Wait! Did Hermes know where he trapped us?"

"I don't think so," the princess says. "But this gives us a secure place to work on balancing the urtar stone."

"Always the bright side," Pemphredo says.

"Dad," Elis says, tapping his bracelet. "Did you see? We got Ora back!"

"Hold on," Anton says, "let me pull over. Show me Elis. Oh, thank goodness. Wait, what's happened to Ora's hair. Please tell me that's a wig."

"Sorry dad," Elis answers, wrapping a supportive arm around Ora. "She's safe. That's what matters most, right?"

"Right," Anton says. "Where are you now?"

"Princess Danae believes this is the room her father created to trap her."

"When are you?" Anton asks, tapping the watch. "Uh… The date and time on the watch are um..."

"What does he mean date and time?" Princess Danae asks, joining the children.

"The watch dials to the date and time of whom he is seeking," Zana says. "That's how they found us when Perseus and the witch took us."

"We don't exactly have a calendar down here, dad," Elis says. "What does the watch say?"

"That can't be right," Anton mutters.

"Dad," Elis says.

"The date is tomorrow."

Elis frowns. "We are in the future."

Princess Danae nods. "That explains the immense amount of dust covering every surface. What year is it?"

172

Emit cocks his head to the side. "In our time? 2027."

"It's been almost two thousand years," says the princess.

"What?" Zana and Ora ask in unison.

"I'm from your past," Princess Danae says, gesturing to Pemphredo. "We are from the first century, year ninety-three."

"Elis?" Anton says, pulling back on to the road.

"I'm here," Elis says.

"I'm about ten minutes from the Mokset hills leading up to the castle. Ermal is going to hike up with me. If you get a hold of anyone at the castle, let them know we are on the way and will wait at the ember archway."

"Who is Ermal?" Princess Danae asks.

"My dad's best friend and a local cop," Emit says.

"Oh, the one that fancies my sister Enyo," Pemphredo says.

Elis covers Emit's ears and glances over at the girls who are giggling. "They are seven."

Pemphredo shrugs.

Elis releases Emit.

"Hey, what was that for?" Emit asks, glaring at Elis. "I don't think Ermal is that fancy."

Elis shakes his head and presses his bracelet. "Be careful and avoid the rocky path up."

"I will," Anton says. "Call me the second you need anything at all."

"Love you."

"Love you too, son."

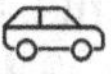

Elis sighs and looks around the room. "I don't suppose you have a stash of food that could have survived a couple thousand years?"

Emit groans. "No food?"

"Ember," the princess mutters. "A little help here, please."

The light hovering overhead brightens to a blinding white. They shield and close their eyes at once.

The air shifts and twirls around their feet.

"What's happening?" Zana asks, holding her hair down.

Ora and Emit huddle together. The wind roars, and the ground rumbles under foot. Elis kneels and places a hand on either side of the hourglass.

Pemphredo lunges forward covering Zana. Princess Danae releases a barrier shield. It wraps them in a clear bubble.

"Keep your eyes shut!" the princess yells over the howling wind.

BANG

Pemphredo cracks open an eye. "No way."

The entire space is gleamingly clean. A long, dark wooden table with two long matching benches is covered in dishes with fresh food.

"The dust is gone!" Elis says, looking around. "Food!"

Emit releases Ora. "Really?" He jumps up and runs for the table. He bounces back off an invisible barrier landing on his butt. "What the…"

"Sorry," the princess says, helping Emit to his feet. "I put up a shield to block us from the wind."

Emit reaches out until his finger stops. "Whoa. You have superpowers?"

"I have a gift from Ember, like you do," the princess says. "You can move time—I can shield people or objects from harm."

"Cool," Emit says, nodding.

The princess releases the shield. "Go on, get some food. It's getting late and it looks like Ember has provided more than just a table full of food." She points to the corner at the two bunk covered beds with fresh linens and a few pillows on each.

"Bunk beds!" Zana squeals.

Pemphredo and Princess Danae laugh.

"Elis when you're done eating," Pemphredo says, pointing down at the hourglass, "we should get started on this."

Elis swallows a bite. "Sure thing."

37

Pemphredo pats her long dark curls dry as she walks to the table. "Elis, please bring the hourglass over here and set it between us." She points to the miniature scale at the far end of the table. "Zana, bring that over and sit across from Elis and I."

"Careful," Princess Danae says, following Elis to the table.

Pemphredo sighs and smiles when he manages to set it down without a grain moving inside. "Great job, Elis! Ora and Emit, let's have you stand on either side of Zana."

Emit drags his feet over to Zana and slumps. "I'm so tired."

Ora yawns and steps beside Zana.

The group yawns in response.

"Sorry," Ora says.

"It's late," Princess Danae says. She stands beside Ora. "We'll get some rest very soon."

"Now," Pemphredo says, "my sisters and I have been researching how to remove the urtar stone that is stuck inside the hourglass. It's important that no one touches it. If it falls, let it fall."

Elis frowns. "Why?"

"It's like the feathered cloaks inside the castle," Pemphredo says. "It will vanish on contact with anyone who touches it."

"Will it put you to sleep until a prince comes to wake you up?" Ora asks.

Pemphredo frowns.

"A sleeping beauty reference," Elis says.

Pemphredo raises a single eyebrow.

"Aurora pricks her finger on a spindle and falls asleep until a prince kisses her," Zana says.

"Um," Pemphredo says, "no, that is not the purpose of the urtar stone. It is the moral compass for humanity."

"Um," Emit says, raising a hand. "What's a moral compass?"

"Your parents have taught you the difference between right and wrong," Pemphredo says.

The kids nod.

"The urtar stone is the stone of judgement. The balance of right and wrong, good and bad, and so on."

"It's a burden too heavy for a normal person to carry," Princess Danae says. "It's literally the weight of the world on their back."

"Alrighty," Elis says, holding up both hands. "No touching."

"Do you three agree?" Pemphredo asks, looking at Emit, Zana, and Ora.

They nod in unison.

Ora raises her hand. "How do we stack the stone against our own?"

"Where did you hear that phrase?" Pemphredo asks.

"From our dreams," Elis says, nodding at Ora. "The rest of the phrase was a compass to guide is near inside. To begin again or tip the end. You must decide."

"That was the message from the Anubis scale," Pemphredo says.

"We've had similar dreams for years," Elis says, gesturing to Ora. "After arriving at the Castle of Teskom, it became clear the messages were from Ember."

"Do you know what it means?" Princess Danae asks.

Pemphredo nods. "The ruby around Xena's neck was supposed to be used to balance the urtar stone on the scale."

"Then why are we messing with it here and now?" Elis asks.

"I've seen this in a vision," Pemphredo says. "I can see the future like you have visions in your dreams."

"You knew we would end up here?" Emit asks, scrunching up his nose.

"Not exactly," Pemphredo says. "I see glimpses of events and when it plays out in real time, I connect the dots."

"So, this is safe?" Princess Danae asks, catching a flicker of light out of the corner of her eye. She turns and a door appears in the middle of the chamber.

Hermes enters through the door and a large man follows him.

"Who is that?" Zana screeches.

"Zana," Hermes says, gesturing to the man beside him. "This is my father, Zeus."

"Right on time," Pemphredo says.

Princess Danae walks to Zeus's side. "He's also my husband."

"Wait!" Elis says. He points to Pemphredo then to Hermes. "You knew they were coming."

Pemphredo winks.

"You're like my million times over great grandpa!" Emit says, skipping over to Zeus.

Zeus smiles and pats Emit's thick brown hair. "And you are Emit?"

"You know my name?" Emit rolls up on his toes and bounces back to his heels.

Zeus smiles and glances over at Ora. "And this is your sister, Ora, I presume."

Ora's mouth falls open.

Elis and Zana glance down at the hourglass between them.

Pemphredo locks eyes with Zeus. "Are you ready?"

Princess Danae glares at Pemphredo. "What are you two planning?"

"It was a back-up plan only," Pemphredo says. "We don't have the Anubis scale or the ruby."

"Right," the princess says, looking at Zeus. "And your role in this scenario is..."

Zeus circles the table and stops beside Elis. "Absorb the urtar stone and bait Chronos."

Princess Danae points at Zeus. "No! Absolutely not."

"It's a good plan," Hermes says, stepping between the princess and Zeus.

"Don't start," the princess says, pushing past Hermes. "I need details. But it's late and for the kids' sake make it quick."

Emit shuffles over to the table beside Ora. Hermes joins Pemphredo, Zeus and Elis.

Pemphredo points to the hourglass. "The chances of finding a balance for the urtar stone without the actual Anubis scale and ruby are zero." She glances at Elis. "In my visions, Elis tips the end of the hourglass until the sand drains to one side, leaving only the stone on the other." She holds up four fingers. "And our four worlds become one." She drops three fingers. "The other part of the visions shows your kind husband touching the urtar stone to lure Chronos towards a portal to the helix from inside the hedge maze."

"The original trap?" Leon asks, calling his staff.

The footage freezes on a young Elis, frowning at the hourglass.

"Zeus absorbs the urtar stone," Elis says.

"How?" Kaly asks.

"We'll get into that in a minute," Elis says. "What's important now is that we set the portals to the helix at each of the twelve doorways."

"The attraction to the urtar stone will be undeniable," Zana says. "Zeus plans to allow Chronos to take the urtar stone. It's our job to make sure Chronos is pushed through a portal the second he takes the stone."

"Will that work?" Itra asks.

"Deino and I can slow him down," Enyo says. "She's waiting up on the parapet."

Danae whirls. "Did you find anything in the archives?"

Enyo nods. "The urtar stone is not just the stone of judgement."

"It's a magnet," Zana says.

"Yes," Enyo says.

"Care to fill us in?" Itra asks, looking between Enyo and Zana.

"You've heard the phrase the worlds will bend and fold," Zana says.

Itra nods.

"If the urtar stone is dropped over a specific ley line, it will change the magnetic force of space between dimensions." Zana holds up four fingers spread apart. Then she drops three fingers. "Dropping the veils would reveal only one world."

"Where is that ley line?" Leon asks.

Zana drops her finger and points down.

"Why would Zeus attempt this?" Kaly asks.

Danae wraps her arm around Itra. "And why bring it here?"

"Mom," Emit says. "They all end the same." He wipes a falling tear from Danae's cheek. "One world."

Danae shakes her head. "And Ora?"

38

Ora appears next to Xena.

Xena looks up from the book on her lap and cocks her head to the side. She studies the face staring back at her. "Ora?"

"Yes," Ora says. "How are you, Xena?"

"Old and frail, it appears," Xena says, holding up her bony, wrinkled hand.

"Where are we?" Ora asks, looking around at the enormous library of bookshelves going off in every direction.

"This is the archives," Xena says.

"Mom, who are you talking to?" Pem asks, winding her way back towards the center of the archives.

"Ora," Xena says.

"Really?" Avi asks from the far side of the enormous hall.

"Yes," Ora says, lifting an eyebrow at Xena.

"That's Avi," Xena says.

"Ora!" Pem says, racing towards her. She halts and looks her over. "Your hair is white."

"I know," Ora says. "We have that in common." She points to Pem's mostly white head of hair.

"Do you know what happened?" Pem asks, running a hand through her hair.

"Chronos trapped you and the family here for thirty years."

"Oh!" Avi says, stepping around some shelves and catching sight of Ora for the first time. "You're all grown up!"

Ora nods. "Hi Avi. How long has it felt for you?"

"A few hours," Avi says, shaking her head. "It's really been thirty years?"

"I'm afraid so," Ora says. "And while it's felt like hours for you, Elis, Emit, Zana and I have lived the full thirty years outside of the castle."

"Oh my," says Xena.

"Did Anton become a single dad of four?" Pem asks.

"He took custody of Emit," Ora says. "I stayed with Princess Danae."

"And Zana?" Avi asks.

"She spent summers with Emit and Elis," Ora says. "But she was with Kaly's mom during the school year."

Xena nods. "Is Kaly's mom still alive?"

Ora shakes her head. "She died of a stroke about eight years ago."

Xena wipes the corner of her eyes. "We've missed so much."

Ora nods. "It's not been easy." She looks around. "What are you guys looking for down here?"

"A way to turn back the last three decades," Xena says.

"Oh," Ora says. "You think that's possible?"

"We hope so," Avi says.

"How can I help?" Ora asks.

"The archives are thought provoked," Xena says. "Like the library off the dining hall. Think of a subject and the book will come towards you." She gestures to the stack of books next to her chair.

"Or you can try wandering the stacks for inspiration," Avi says. "I think I am going to work through the stack here."

"I'll take a wander this way," Pem says. "Oh, and if a book has blank pages, just say the word 'hapur'. If it remains blank, Ember has it hidden for a reason."

"Got it." Ora walks down an aisle, running her hand over the spines of the books. *The question is, can we reverse time.*

She circles the maze of shelves for twenty minutes, picking up books as she walks. Then she heads back towards the center.

"I've got something," Xena says, calling over her shoulder.

"You're sure?" Ora pulls her long white hair away from her face and looks over Xena's shoulder.

Xena points to the small text under a pastel illustration of Chronos on bended knee in front of a glowing woman. "Here, take a look."

Ora studies the illustration and strains her eyes to read the text. "I think I need reading glasses, but you're right. This may be our only lead."

"I hope it's something," Avi says. She eyes the stack of books as tall as Pem sitting on the matching armchair. "The archive's enormous collection appears to be somewhat lacking in answers for the reversal of three decades."

"We're listening," Pem says, setting aside her own book.

Xena nods and clears her throat. "You must appear to his heart, appeal to his ego, and he will bow. Her vow will call his fall to part his bind over time."

"It's a bit vague." Pem throws her head back and glances up at the dome. "Is that supposed to be Leon?"

Ora spots the stained-glass panel of a man with a scythe. "My word, and is that my mom?"

The next stained-glass panel is a woman holding two babies, one wrapped in a blue cloth and the other wrapped in a gold cloth.

Xena wobbles as she stands. Her frail body stoops forward. She pats Ora on the shoulder. "I believe so."

Ora wipes a falling tear away and catches the glint of gold on her left hand. She stares at the simple gold band wrapped around her ring finger. She swallows a sob expanding in her chest and bites down on her quivering lower lip.

Avi stands and stretches. "Do you think we should get back on task?"

"Yes," Xena says, "I believe we need to find a copy of this vow."

"Kaly read a vow before everything went sideways," Ora says.

A book from the stack between Pem and Avi shoots out and opens in front of Ora.

"Thanks Ember," Ora says, reaching for the book. She examines the page. "To end your reign, I break my vow. To start again, you must bow. Until then, it ends with me. By my line, I banish thee, time, to the helix for infinity." She points to the edge of the page. "One problem." She turns the book towards the others. "I can't translate the writing on the edge, but maybe Kaly can. I recognize a few symbols. Possibly ancient Greek?"

Xena narrows her eyes and studies the page. "I think this may be Illyrian."

"Teuta," Pem says. "We need a lift."

"Wait," Ora says, as they vanish.

Ora bends at the waist until she catches her breath. She straightens and pulls back her white curls. Her eyes meet Danae's wide eyes.

"Ora," Danae whispers.

Itra whirls around and runs towards Ora. He scoops her up.

"Hi dad," Ora says, handing off the books to Pem.

Itra chuckles. "Love you too, princess."

Ora stiffens. "You know?" Ora's eyes land on Emit.

Emit gives a quick shake of his head.

Itra sets her down.

Danae rushes to her. "Ora, my girl." She wraps her in a hug.

"Hi mom," Ora says, releasing Danae. "You look well... considering."

Danae strokes Ora's long white curls. "I'm so sorry."

Ora shakes her head. "We've never blamed you for any of this." She turns to Elis and Zana. "You said you would tell them it wasn't their fault."

Elis and Zana glance at each other.

"We haven't gotten there yet," Zana whispers.

"What do you mean?" Danae asks, turning with her arm draped over Ora.

"Aunt Xena," Kaly says, pulling out a chair. "Please sit. You look faint."

"Thirty years has not been kind to an already old woman," Xena says, sitting in the offered chair.

Danae stares at Zana. "What does Ora mean?"

"I was taken from them," Ora says.

"But we saw Hermes and Pemphredo find you," Danae says.

"For the sake of time," Emit says, "we had to leave Ora behind."

"What?" Danae asks. Her eyes flick from Emit to Ora.

"It was the only way," Ora says.

"I don't understand," Danae whispers.

Ora frowns. "My gift to reverse time made it impossible for me to step through the portal back to Anton's apartment."

Teuta gasps.

All eyes focus on Teuta.

"I saw you there," Teuta says, pointing at Ora. "You were a teenager. I was trapped in the City of Time right before Prende took me to the fairies on the mountain."

Ora nods. "I was in hiding and you just appeared in my quarters."

"I thought it was a dream," Teuta says.

Danae grips Ora's hand. "You were stuck in the City of Time for thirty years?"

"Yes."

"But how, or more importantly, why?" Itra asks. "Ember was supposed to protect them."

"She's been a little tied up trying to slow Chronos down," Ora says.

∞

Chronos drops his arm, it bounces off his hip, and his chest swells.

"Guys!" Junior yells. *"He's moving again."*

Leon stands. "We've got movement."

"The doorways are opening," Junior says, pacing the landing. *"What now?"*

"It's Hermes!" Zana says, grabbing Elis's arm.

"Maybe," Elis says.

"Care to fill us in?" Kaly asks.

"Our plan," Zana says. "We were about to get to that in the playback.

"No time for that now," Emit says.

"Then you all had better tell us what the plan is fast!" Itra asks.

"Right," Elis says. "If the doors open and Zeus steps through—we have an opportunity to set our trap."

39

"Ember," Chronos whispers. "Come out." He weaves his way through the hedge maze. "I'm running out of patience."

"So, why are you running?"

Chronos stops and slowly turns.

The outline of a woman appears near the statue in the center.

"She's showing herself," Junior says, peering out the window.

"Ember is showing herself to Chronos," Leon says. "If we are going to act, we need to do it now."

"You have to set a portal to the helix at every door," Elis says, grabbing Leon's arm. "It's our only chance."

"Where's Pem?" Xena says, looking around. "And Teuta?"

"Pem was here a second ago." Avi pins her eyes on Xena. "She wouldn't, would she?"

Xena's mouth falls open.

"Deino," Enyo says. *"Is that Pem acting as Ember?"*

"She wouldn't dare," Deino says, squinting down at the second figure in the hedge maze.

"Teuta," Leon says.

Teuta appears next to Leon.

"Where's Pem?" Xena asks, marching towards Teuta.

"Distracting Chronos," Teuta says, sticking her chin out. "Protect and serve."

Leon steps between Xena and Teuta. "Look I know more than anyone how much you would like to sucker punch her, but we need to move quickly and quietly."

Xena's nostrils flare, but she nods and steps back.

Leon turns his back to Xena. "Trust me, I will not stop her next time."

Teuta's face falters from smirk to frown.

"Put me close to the wall out of sight of Chronos," Leon says. He vanishes.

Ora comes to Xena's side and helps her back to the table.

"Where's that book?" asks Xena.

Ora points to the corner of the table.

"Did you find something important?" Danae asks.

Ora nods. "We found an illustration of Chronos bending his knee in front of the figure of a glowing woman. And we were hoping Kaly could translate the remaining text."

"Can you show me?" Kaly asks, examining the books.

Ora nods and picks up the slim volume. She thumbs through the pages until she spots the pastels. "The passage here is where we need your assistance." She hands the book to Kaly.

Kaly hovers her finger above the page and traces the text. "This is ancient Illyrian." She sets the book down. A pen and paper appear next to the book. "I've been working with Vincent on this language over the last several years."

"Uncle Vincent," Itra whispers. He turns to Emit. "Is he—"

"He's been gone about twenty years," Emit says.

"Oh dear," Danae says, hugging Itra.

"I never got to say goodbye," Ora whispers.

"Ora," Itra says. "I'm so sorry."

Itra releases Danae and goes to Ora. He hugs her and nods towards the paper Kaly is holding. "Tell me good news."

Kaly sighs. "I have translated most of it, but in true Ember fashion it's a bit of a riddle."

Itra rubs a hand over his scruffy beard. "Ugh, of course."

"Let's hear it," Ora says, arms wrapped around Itra's waist.

"Hear my plea on your knee. Resign thy space and I will lace time to my line. Keep thy space and I will end our time."

Xena laughs. "I would say that's not a riddle. It sounds more like an ultimatum."

Leon peeks over a hedge and spots Chronos's head and shoulders slowly moving towards the center. *Damn, he's tall.* He ducks down and calls his staff, double tapping it so the scythe extends. Staying low, he moves to the first doorway. He risks a second glance over the hedge and immediately ducks back down.

Chronos is embracing a glowing woman in the center of the maze.

"I'm in position," Leon says. *"If he moves an inch, tell me!"*

"I have eyes from up here," Deino says, peering around the stone column. *"Go!"*

Leon doesn't hesitate and swings the scythe straight down through the first doorway. He pokes his head through. His eyes focus on a space full of twisting lights and mirrored floors. He pulls his head out and shakes it until the spots clouding his vision clear.

188

"One down, eleven to go." Leon moves silently into the maze. *"Help me navigate."*

Deino peeks over the edge. *"Left, two rights and a left."*

Leon follows her instructions and finds the second passage. He repeats the swipe with his scythe.

Deino guides him to five doors and is about to say the last two turns when movement makes her pause.

"He's stepping away from the woman," Junior says.

Leon crouches low. *Not even halfway.* *"Can I keep going?"*

"Leon, is it?" Chronos calls out.

"Shit!" Leon mutters.

"Finish the seven portals," Deino says, *"we'll slow him down."*

"We?" Leon asks.

Enyo appears next to Leon. She blocks the swing of his scythe with her sword. "Easy!"

"Sorry," Leon mutters. "What's the plan?"

"Just keep moving."

"Two lefts, one right," Deino says.

Leon nods and takes off.

Enyo charges through the maze towards the center.

"Andromeda," Junior says.

Enyo freezes near the opening to the center. *"Where?"*

"Two doorways down from where Leon is now," Junior says, edging closer to the window. *"Deino, can you see her?"*

"She's moving towards the center," Deino says, running to the next stone column. *"Avi, stand by for an all call to the maze."*

"Noted," Avi responds in thought and aloud. She stands from the dining hall table and motions to Kaly.

Xena's boney hand shakes as she points at Avi. "Are we going in?"

"Soon," Avi says, gripping her infinity charm.

"But you're not going anywhere," Kaly says, squaring her shoulders to Xena. "You must be in your eighties now!"

"More like nineties, I'm ninety-two!" Xena says. She sighs and sits back down.

Zana wraps an arm around Xena.

"Exactly," Kaly says, folding her arms. "You have no business being in the fray. We've got this."

"You sound just like your father," Xena says. "My brother was always so bossy."

Kaly smirks. "I'll take that as a compliment."

"As you should."

"I feel another person coming," Danae says.

"Zeus is here!" Junior says. *"He just came out of the same doorway as Andromeda."*

"Wait, does that mean she's on our side?" Leon says.

"Avi, can you ask one of the children..." Deino says.

"Children, hah," Avi says. She turns to the group in the dining hall. "So, can Andromeda be trusted?"

"Absolutely," says Ora, turning to Zana. "You didn't tell them?"

"Like I said, we never got a chance to tell them the whole story," says Zana.

"Relaying the message," says Avi. *"Andromeda is to be trusted, I repeat, Andromeda is to be trusted."*

Leon groans from his position in the maze.

"Alright, Avi, send us inside," Deino says.

"It's time," Avi says. *"We could use an extra set of eyes from the parapet to help us navigate the maze."*

Itra nods. "On my way."

Avi closes her eyes and pictures Kaly, Deino, and herself inside the hedge maze.

Xena leans against Zana and whispers, "I hope this works."

190

40

Chronos narrows his eyes on the glowing woman. "We have company?"

The woman keeps his gaze. "Yes."

Chronos smirks. "You never could lie."

"Goddess of knowledge, not tricks or deception."

Chronos's eyes dart to the window.

Junior ducks away.

"A new pet like Leon?" Chronos muses.

"A guardian of sorts," she says, waving a hand to Enyo to keep out of sight.

Enyo sinks back down. *"Pem's got his attention. Leon, how many more?"*

"Three," Leon says, swiping his scythe down through the ninth doorway. He steps back inside the maze. *"Deino, directions?"*

"I'm inside the maze now," Deino says.

"I've taken her place though, Leon," Itra says. *"Three lefts, two rights and a left."*

Leon moves silently through the maze.

"Hold!" Junior shouts.

Leon skids to a stop. He waits, but a scuffle of footsteps to his right draws his attention. He flattens himself against the hedge and readies his scythe.

"My, my, and who do we have here," Chronos says, dragging Kaly into the center.

"Get your hands off of me!" Kaly says.

"Leon, don't move!" Enyo commands. *"We've got this."*

"Like hell," Leon says.

"Finish the trap," Kaly says. *"This is part of the plan."*

"Dammit!" He exhales. *"Don't do anything stupid."*

Leon makes it to the tenth doorway and freezes mid swipe.

A man emerges from the shadows.

Leon looks the man over—moppy brown curls fall over a familiar face. Then Leon notices his winged shoes. "Hermes?"

Hermes holds a finger to his lips.

"Why are you hiding?" Leon whispers, staring Hermes down.

"I'm part of the plan," Hermes whispers.

"Chronos," Zeus says, stepping out of the maze near the center.

"Go time," Hermes says, stepping out of the shadows and into the maze.

Leon swipes the doorway with his scythe. He turns to run back into the maze.

Hermes grabs his shoulder.

Leon holds up two fingers and motions towards the other doorways. "I still have two left."

"Wait until they start talking," Hermes whispers.

"And you are?" Chronos says, turning to face Zeus. Hermes nods and Leon moves towards the last two doors. "Oh, I see. The urtar stone has a new host." He shrugs and smirks. "Clever." He looks over his shoulder. "Was this your... who the hell are you?"

Pem freezes mid transformation from the glowing woman back to her own skin. She gives a slight bow and finishes her transformation.

Chronos drops Kaly's arm.

Kaly staggers back out of his reach.

"Where is Ember?" Chronos asks.

"Here," Enyo says, stepping out of the maze.

"Here," Avi says, stepping out of the maze across from Kaly.

"Here," Deino says. She steps between Kaly and Pem.

"Here," Andromeda says, stepping between Deino and Enyo.

"Leon?" Enyo calls.

"One more," Leon says, wiping the sweat from his forehead. He shuffles back into the maze. *"Hermes is here."*

"Good," Enyo says, drawing her dagger and sword.

Chronos raises his arms out to his side. "You think you have me surrounded?" His feet lift off the sandy ground.

Hermes flies up and over Chronos.

Chronos twitches a finger. Hermes loses altitude, turning headfirst towards the ground.

Andromeda raises her hand, adorned again with several rings. She twists her wrist until Hermes slowly turns right side up.

Hermes winks and grins at Chronos's his fallen smirk.

"You have two choices," Zeus says, gaining Chronos's attention once again. "Surrender to us or have eternal bliss with Ember."

"And the second option is…" Chronos says, lowering his feet back to the ground. "Because surrendering is eternal bliss with Ember."

"I didn't say what you were surrendering," Zeus says.

"Done!" Leon yells.

"Danae," Itra says, *"Leon has set all the portals."*

Danae taps the table between Emit and Ora. "The portal traps are set. Do you know what they plan to do next?"

Emit nods. "Is Hermes there?"

"He is," Junior says, from the open doorway to the conservatory. He wheezes and coughs.

"Are you ok?" Danae asks, jogging to Junior's side.

"I think I need Dita's help," Junior says, coughing again.

"Are you sick?" Danae asks.

Junior nods.

"Is she still in the present cavern watching Perseus?" Danae asks.

"I hope so," Junior says, "but she hasn't answered my last few requests for updates."

"Teuta," Danae says.

Teuta appears beside Danae. "Check on Dita!"

"She's gone," Teuta says.

"Gone where?" Junior asks, fighting to catch his breath.

"Perseus collapsed after complaining of chest pain a few minutes ago," Teuta says. "I brought her a cloak and she flew out of the cavern to the revolutionary ember archway."

"Bring her back," Junior whispers, falling to his knees. "I can't..." His eyes roll back, and he slumps before his large frame teeters towards the floor.

Teuta slides under him and catches his head in her lap. "Junior." She shakes his shoulders. "Don't you dare drop dead now!"

41

"Danae?" Itra says, watching Hermes circle above Chronos.

"Junior collapsed," Danae says. *"Dita left to check on Perseus."*

"Oh, that's not good," Itra says. *"We've got action inside the maze."*

"Do they need help?" Danae asks, trying to find Junior's pulse. She prods his wrists and finds a faint thump that presses against her fingers.

"No, stay put."

Xena comes to Danae's side. "What can I do?"

"Keep them here," Danae whispers, eying Emit and Elis edging closer to the door to the conservatory. "He's got a pulse, but it's faint." She glances up at Teuta's face.

Teuta wipes the tears streaming down her cheeks with her free hand. "He's alive?"

"Yes," Danae says, "for now." She stands and helps Xena to her feet. Together, they block the door to the conservatory. "Elis, please tell us what the endgame is here."

Elis pulls at his collar. "Hermes explained it as a strategic game of cat and mouse."

"Zeus releases the urtar stone and the sisters dangle it as bait for Chronos," Emit says.

"But the only way to release the urtar stone is the hourglass or death," Xena says, shaking her head. "I imagine you had to break the hourglass, right?"

Elis nods. "Chronos needs to merge with the urtar stone in order for the helix to hold him."

"Merge how?" Danae asks. "At the cost of Zeus?"

Emit and Elis glance at Zana. She nods.

"Zeus will die," Zana says. "It's a fate he's known for decades."

"Die by whose hand?" Xena asks. Her eyes dance between Elis and Emit who are avoiding her gaze.

"Ember," Teuta says, shifting Junior's head. "She will take Zeus's life."

"Then what?" Danae asks. "Are we next?"

"No mom," Emit says. "The plan is to merge and balance."

"With this," Ora says, holding the Anubis scale. "Ember will fill one side, Chronos and the stone will fill the other."

Xena frowns and palms the ruby still dangling from the gold chain around her neck. "Explain how."

Zana waves her hand around. "Everything here is Ember, right?"

Xena glances at Danae. "Sure."

"Beginning with the Castle of Teskom," Zana says, "Ember's goal was to protect the knowledge of the world in one place. But the three dimensions of parallel time were created Ember and Chronos, not just her alone."

Danae looks down at Teuta. "Something you kindly left out of the welcome packet."

Teuta averts her eyes. "It wasn't relevant at the time."

Zana continues. "Chronos grew bored with observing the three worlds and wanted to drop the veils to cause chaos and destruction for pure entertainment."

"Boredom," Xena scoffs, "a common cause of evil."

Zana smirks. "To true. But Ember tried to resolve his angst, using the ancient urtar stone to balance the morality of Chronos."

"Ember thought she could quell his true nature," Xena whispers.

⚖️

"Ember!" Chronos bellows, circling the fairy statue.

"Yes," the women answer in unison.

Chronos kicks the ground spewing bits of gravel and sand into Andromeda's face. She doesn't flinch.

"Enough with the games!" Chronos yells.

Zeus takes a step towards Chronos. "Let's begin."

Chronos squares his shoulders and steps towards Zeus.

Enyo, Deino, Avi, Pem, and Kaly take a step forward.

Andromeda follows their lead and joins the circle.

Hermes slowly descends closer to Chronos, keeping out of his line of sight.

Zeus takes another step and Chronos matches his movement until they are a few feet apart.

"You realize your time is over," Chronos says, staring Zeus down.

"Of course, I do," Zeus says and winks. "And so is yours." He looks up. "I'm ready."

Zeus falls to his knees. His face turns a sickly shade of green before morphing to a dark purple. He lets out a final puff of air before his body slumps to the side with a deafening thud of thunder.

The air around Zeus spins, kicking up a twister of dirt. It abruptly stops when Chronos opens his hand. The urtar stone falls from the debris into Chronos's palm. The shimmery form of Chronos becomes solid in an instant.

Hermes descends the final few feet and slaps a gold cuff across Chronos's forearm. The cuff vanishes on contact, leaving a tattoo in its place.

Chronos yanks his arm away and examines the fresh mark. "You fool!" He points a finger at Hermes hovering across from him. "You think this will hold the god of time and space?"

"Hold, no. Control, maybe."

Chronos laughs and waves his hand.

Hermes flies back, holding his gut, but he slows just before crashing into the stone wall.

Andromeda drops her hand when Chronos turns towards her.

Hermes plops on top of the hedge and lets his legs dangle over the edge. He begins slowly clapping. "Bravo!"

"What did you do?" Chronos asks, inspecting the ink on his forearm. He rubs his arm.

The women, except for Andromeda, step forward, raising their arms and starting a chant. "Unravel the weave and hear us breathe. Bind our line to protect time, our legacy thine. Hear our call. Bind us all. Yield the fall." A push of air twirls around their feet.

"Stop!" Chronos yells.

They continue. "Bring us light to guide the night. To protect and rewind the ember in time, Illyria of mine."

The sky fades to black.

The air around their feet pushes up, surrounding Chronos in twirling dust.

His hand reaches out of the twister blasting a gust towards Kaly and Deino.

Andromeda holds her hand up, palm out.

The gust redirects towards Chronos—knocking him off balance. He stumbles into the fairy statue and his feet leave the ground. He reaches and claws at the stone. He finally grasps the head of Medusa. His long white beard hangs down blocking his view of the ground.

"Hermes, when we drop our arms," Enyo says. *"We have one shot to hurl him into one of the helix traps."*

198

"Andromeda," Hermes says, *"be ready to counter his moves."*

"We've got this!" Andromeda says.

"We're ready," Hermes says.

"Ember, in three, two, one…" Enyo says.

The women drop their arms.

The air explodes in a wave around them, bending the hedges near their roots.

Hermes topples backwards.

"Now!" Andromeda yells, ducking her head and holding up her hands.

Chronos loses his grip on Medusa's head. He spins head over heels, grazing the tops of the hedges. He collides with the stonewall above one of the open passageways.

The stones crack and crumble around Chronos.

Hermes staggers to his feet.

"I can't hold him forever!" Andromeda yells.

Chronos strains against the hold of Andromeda's magic. Pressed against the crumbling stones, he pries two fingers from the wall.

Hermes flies straight up and levels himself across from Chronos. "Release!"

Chronos looks up for an arrow hurtling in his direction but is surprised when gravity drops him.

Hermes flies across the maze, landing his two feet on the chest of Chronos.

The kick sends Chronos through the open portal. The portal seals and the gold cuff and the urtar stone fall to the ground in front of the doorway.

"Whoop!" Hermes holds up his fist. "It worked. He's gone!"

Leon barrels through the maze. "Kaly!"

Kaly remains fixated on the crumpled form of where Zeus had once stood. His large body had been reduced to a pile of ash.

Leon wraps her in a hug. "Are you hurt?"

"No," Kaly whispers, hugging him back. "Is it really over?"

"I think so," Leon says, leaning back to look her over. "Because you're young again."

Kaly shakes her head and blinks twice. "Oh! And you are too!" She scratches his dark brown stubble. "And the kids?"

"We'll have to see if we can call them that anymore."

Kaly frowns. "True."

Hermes lands beside Leon. He looks over his father's ashes and bows his head.

Leon puts a comforting hand on his shoulder. "I'm sorry Hermes."

Hermes nods. "His sacrifice was admirable."

Andromeda, Enyo, and Deino come to stand next to Hermes.

"Zeus knew the outcome would be this?" Pem asks, joining the others.

Hermes nods.

Pem whispers, "Ashes to ashes, dust to dust—literally."

Andromeda slowly waves her hand over the pile. The ashes bounce and rise to take the ashy shape of a standing Zeus. She nods to Enyo, solemnly.

"Mold and make," Enyo says, joining hands with Deino. "In his shape. Hear us call, Ember divine, make this man a shrine."

A rush of air blows past Kaly and Leon.

Kaly gazes up at the towering stone statue of Zeus that now stands over her.

"How?" Leon asks.

"Whoa," Pem says, circling the statue. "I didn't know we could do that?"

"You can't," Enyo says, releasing Deino's hand.

"Not without me at least," Andromeda says.

"Still a witch," Leon glares at Andromeda. "You kidnapped our kids, took Ora again, and showed up here anyway, knowing we would likely split you in two—ballsy."

Andromeda smirks. "It's not wise to scorn your allies a third time."

"Allies?" Leon asks, straightening his stance and staring her down. "Is that what we are now?"

Enyo stands. "She did just hold back a god to help us out."

Leon rolls his eyes. "I'm pretty sure that fancy skill was abused in this very place once before." He points to her hands. "How did you get your precious jewels back?"

"They were forged a-new under Zeus's watchful eye," Andromeda says, standing. "If you'll excuse me, I need to check if my husband's still breathing."

Pem points up to a window. "I believe Dita has a gift for you."

Dita waves, holding up a barely conscious Perseus.

Andromeda whispers, "Perseus."

42

"Danae," Itra says, running into the dining hall.

The dining hall is empty.

He continues towards the Zeus war room. It's vacant.

"Danae!" He starts up the steps to the suites. "Where the hell did everyone go?"

"Dad!"

Itra stops mid step and slowly turns around. "Ora?" He blinks and his mouth falls open. His seven-year-old daughter stares up at him. "How?"

Ora cocks her head to the side. "What do you mean, daddy?"

Itra squats down on the step in front of her. He shakes his head and pushes a white curl back from her face. "Do you know where your mom is?"

Ora nods. "Emit and Elis wanted to see something called a Mui war room." She shrugs and turns to walk down the steps. "I heard you yell mom's name, so I came out to find you."

Itra swallows and stands. He follows her out of the Zeus war room and back into the dining hall.

Emit emerges from the door leading to the Mui war room. "Dad, did you see the spiral stairs?"

Itra kneels to the ground, his breath coming in slow short gasps.

Danae and Elis are laughing when they enter the dining hall.

"Itra!" Danae runs towards him. "What's wrong?"

"They're..." Itra says, gasping for a full breath, "...kids again."

"Ora was able to turn back time," Danae whispers. "And they don't remember a thing."

Zana skips into the room from the corridor of portraits with Xena close on her heels.

"Was somebody yelling?" Zana asks.

"My dad," Ora says. "He's acting funny."

Itra sits back and puts his head between his knees.

"Just breathe," Danae says quietly. "The good news is we just arrived, and the last forty-eight hours never happened for them."

Itra lifts his head. "Seriously?"

Danae nods. "And Anton..."

Anton steps out of the library, holding a book. "Did you know that Mui's parents were from the small village of Selcë?"

"...is thankfully clueless like the kids."

Xena winks at Itra as she passes him to inspect the book Anton is holding.

"She's... not old," Itra says, looking Danae over. "And your hair, it's just brown."

Danae smirks. "I kind of liked the grey."

"I don't understand," Itra says, getting to his feet.

"About ten minutes ago," Danae says, ushering him away from the kids who are busy looking over Anton's shoulder, "we woke up on the floor in the dining hall. Everyone was here except Teuta and Junior."

Itra shakes his head. "And where is Teuta now?"

Danae shakes her head. "She hasn't answered our calls."

"Leon and Kaly?" Itra says, looking around.

"I thought they were with you," Danae says.

"I ran down from the parapet as soon as Hermes kicked Chronos through the portal," Itra says.

"He's gone?" Danae asks.

"Yes," Itra says. "Maybe I should check on the others?"

Danae nods. "Take Xena. Anton and I will look after the kids."

Xena looks up from the book. "What's up?"

"Will you join me in checking on the others," Itra says, nodding towards the conservatory door.

Xena nods and wiggles her way out of the crowd around Anton and the book.

"Is everything ok?" Anton mouths over Zana's head.

Danae nods.

⏱

"I can't believe they managed to turn back time," Itra says, looking over at Xena's wide smile.

The plants sway as they pass through the conservatory towards the front entrance.

"It's a miracle," Xena says, "but I have so many questions."

"You and me both." Itra takes the lead up to the first-floor landing. He peeks out the window. *No movement.* He squints to make out the walls.

"The twelve passageways are closed," Itra says.

"It's too dark." Xena steps to the center of the window, scans the entire hedge maze, and peers up at the dark clouds hovering right over the castle. "Where are they?"

"The last thing I saw on my way down was Leon hugging Kaly."

"And Chronos?" Xena asks.

"Pushed through one of the portals Leon set up," Itra says, standing on his tiptoes. "Does the stone fairy look a little off center to you?"

Xena nods. "Maybe they're returning the cuff to the vault?"

"The keeper's cuff?" Itra asks, dropping back down on his heels.

"Yes."

"Hmm, I saw Hermes strike Chronos with something after Zeus died. It left a mark." Itra points to his forearm. "Who was the keeper?"

"Ora," Xena says.

204

"Are you..." Itra yells.

Xena holds up a hand. "Before you get mad, hear me out."

Itra huffs out a breath. "This had better be good."

"Ora's gift is to rewind time to its origin," Xena explains. "We saw her do this before Chronos arrived when time was stopped outside of the ember archways."

Itra nods.

"And her control of Chronos was the only chance we had to reset the clock—or in our case, turn time back three decades."

"But how?" Itra asks, pacing the landing.

"When Chronos absorbed the urtar stone," Xena says, "his shadow became human. The keeper's cuff gave Ora a chance to use her gift using Chronos and his power over time as a catalyst. The plan was to disable him long enough to allow Ora a chance to rewind time." She grins. "And she did. I still can't believe it worked."

"And you knew all of this beforehand," Itra says. "Why didn't you share this with us when Danae and I were asking?"

Xena frowns. "It was only an option if Zeus showed up and by then everything was moving in real time. Not exactly a great time to pause and explain."

"Humph," Itra says. Then he thinks for a bit. "Pem and I brought up the keeper's cuff with the Anubis scale from the vault. That was right before Chronos showed up. How did it end up with Hermes?"

Xena chuckles. "Emit thought the bag looked cool and took it, not knowing what it was."

Itra slaps his palm against his forehead.

"Pem left it on the table after setting the Anubis scale down," he says.

Then he points his finger at Xena. "So, the scale and the ruby around your neck were all a myth?"

"They were a back-up plan," Xena says, patting the jewel under her top.

43

"Thank you for accompanying Hermes," Princess Danae says, glancing around the large suite filled with many tear-streaked faces. "The City of Time lost its leader today. His life and dedication to Ember will always be remembered." Her watery eyes fixate on the large statue of Zeus standing on her balcony. The wails of mourning villagers below float in through the open doors.

"His sacrifice was not his alone," Leon says. "He joins Iana and Mui in the ranks of heroes who died protecting Ember and the Castle of Teskom."

Princess Danae wipes a falling tear and nods once. "Protect and serve, always seems to come at a cost."

Kaly hugs the princess and whispers, "A debt for Ember to repay."

"A debt," Princess Danae says, a smile tugs the corner of her mouth. "We'll see."

Leon follows Kaly out of the suite. He gently closes the door behind him and Kaly. They walk quietly hand in hand down the stone corridor towards a grand staircase.

Kaly gives Leon's hand a light squeeze. "Do you think we did the right thing?"

"What other option did we have?" Leon asks.

"The scale and the urtar stone," Kaly says. "If Zeus never absorbed the stone, we could have tried to balance it with the ruby."

Leon stops and faces Kaly. "But Chronos would still be inside the Castle of Teskom." He shakes his head. "Who knows the additional damage he could have inflicted on the rest of the worlds beyond the ember archways?"

Kaly shakes out her hands. "The logical part of me agrees... the history professor is screaming at the injustice of Zeus's death."

"He swore an oath to protect and serve Ember and the Castle of Teskom," Leon says, taking her hands. "He did—at the very same cost as Iana."

Kaly frowns. "True." She fiddles with her gold ring. "We should get back."

"Wait," Princess Danae says, rushing down the corridor.

"What's wrong?" Leon asks.

The princess stops in front of Leon and takes a breath. "Zeus was wearing an ember jewel around his neck. It was a time stone to travel to and from the castle freely." She points to Leon's gold ring. "Like your rings."

Leon nods. "Ok."

"I know for sure he was wearing it when he left. Hermes just went out to check that Perendi hasn't been causing any trouble, and I forgot to ask him. Did you find it?"

Leon glances back at Kaly. "Did you see anything like that on the ground of the hedge maze?"

"No," Kaly says. "We'll be sure to look the second we return."

The princess wrings her hands. "If Chronos took it..."

"Understood." Leon takes Kaly's hand.

The princess nods and takes a step back as a door appears to Leon's right. Kaly and Leon rush through the open door.

Enyo helps Dita support Perseus's weight up the set of steps to the Mui suites.

Deino shoulders open the first door she finds. It pops open with a long, loud squeak.

Andromeda runs to the small bed in the center of the room and throws the blankets back.

Enyo and Dita back Perseus up to the edge of the bed.

"Are you okay?" Andromeda says, facing her husband.

Perseus lifts his gaze to her. "Thirsty, but I'll be fine," he says, he reaches up to touch her face. "Your hair... is different."

"You can thank your descendent, the one with the long scythe."

"Let's lay him back," Dita says.

Andromeda fusses with the pillows to support him as Dita and Enyo shift him back and up on the bed.

Deino rounds to the end of the bed. "Do you need supplies?"

"No," Dita says, steadying her hands over his chest. "He seems fine. I did a quick assessment in the cave, but I want to do a thorough one now. Can you and Enyo go check on the others?"

"Of course," Enyo says, stepping out into the corridor. Deino follows her out.

Enyo quickly walks to the steps and down to the landing with the window overlooking the maze. She turns towards Deino. "It's not over."

Deino frowns. "What do you mean?"

Enyo shakes her head. "That was too simple, too easy."

"I don't think anything we did in there," Deino says, pointing to the maze, "was easy."

"Call it intuition or whatever, but I think we need to talk to Pemphredo," Enyo says, rushing down the steps. She swings away from the conservatory and towards the dark spiraling steps.

"Where are you going?" Deino asks, catching up with her.

"To the present cavern."

"But we should check on the others."

Enyo shrugs. "You can go, but I can't shake this feeling."

"Fine, but let's go quickly." Deino follows Enyo down the spiral steps.

Xena sees movement in the maze below. She taps on the glass of window. "Itra! Look, they're back."

Below, Leon calls his staff and taps once. The ember glow gives Kaly light to search.

"*Leon,*" Itra says, watching Kaly kneel and sift through the dirt.

Leon looks up at the window and waves. "*Slight problem. Zeus was wearing an ember jewel around his neck. It's missing.*"

"*Why is that a problem?*" Itra asks.

"*It's like our rings,*" Leon says, holding up his thumb.

"*If Chronos...*" Itra says.

Leon nods.

Itra takes Xena's hand. "Ember, a little help here."

Xena and Itra land in the hedge maze across from Leon and Kaly.

Xena bends and gasps. "A little warning next time." She straightens. "What's got everyone on their hands and knees?"

Kaly blows a hair out of her face and looks up at Xena. "Zeus was wearing an ember jewel with the same properties as our rings," she says, focusing on the dirt in her hands. "If Chronos managed to take it..."

"Say no more," Xena says, dropping to all fours next to Itra.

"Is there a reason why the fairy statue is off center?" Itra asks, shifting a foot over.

"Avi and Pem were returning the urtar stone and keeper's cuff to the vault." Kaly sits back on her heels. "They haven't returned?"

"Not that we know of," Itra says, pointing at the statue. "And the fairy is still off center."

"Pem!" Xena says, crawling over to the opening. She stands and brushes the dirt off her knees. "Pem!"

44

Pem shuffles down the ramp behind Avi. She juggles the urtar stone in its new hourglass. "Why did you think the person responsible for knocking over the old hourglass should carry it down to the vault?"

Avi laughs. "I nearly forgot about that." She looks over her shoulder. "You good?"

"Yeah," Pem says.

Avi pauses at the bottom of the ramp and looks around. "I'll never get over how huge this room is."

The endless space appears to go on for an eternity.

Pem sidles up to Avi. "It's crazy to think that at least sixty percent of the artifacts down here never existed in our dimension."

"Ha," Avi says. "Let's hope neither of these have to come out again." She holds up the gold cuff and gestures to the hourglass. "Leon said there was a chest next to a floating car."

Pem tilts her head to the right. "I think it's across from the Medusa Shield. Fair warning, that shield still creeps me out." She walks to the marble pedestal and gently sets the hourglass down.

"Found it!" Avi says, opening the chest. "Whoa. That's a lot of gold."

Pem walks over to Avi. "Dang, if only we knew whether or not the treasure has any other magical components or curse."

"So true," Avi says, placing the keeper's cuff in a vacant velvet slot. She lowers the lid carefully and a faint click echoes around the space.

"Does that mean it's sealed?" Pem asks.

Avi shrugs. "No idea." She turns and jumps—the writhing snakes surrounding Medusa's head hiss. "You weren't joking. That thing is beyond creepy."

Pem shivers and nudges Avi back towards the ramp. "Let's see how the others are doing."

"Pem?" Avi asks, climbing up onto the ramp.

"Yeah," Pem says, following her up.

"Do you think with the time leap and reset that Noel will remember me?" Avi asks, biting her lower lip.

"Lovesick Noel? Absolutely!"

Avi sighs. "Good."

They reach the top of the ramp and weave their way through the stalagmites back to an opening.

Pem pauses on the uneven stone steps.

Avi looks over her shoulder. "What's wrong?"

"I think my mom just yelled my name," Pem says, bolting past Avi and up the rest of the steps. "Mom!"

"Pem?" Xena calls again.

"We're here," Pem says, jogging down the corridor to the spiral steps.

"Oh, thank goodness," Xena says.

Pem and Avi emerge to furrowed brows and frowns.

"What's happened?" Avi asks, looking at Kaly's dirty knees and hands.

Kaly throws a handful of dirt back to the ground. "Question," she says. "Did either of you see an ember jewel on the ground or on Zeus?"

"No," Avi says, looking at Pem.

Pem shrugs. "No, why?"

"Chronos may have taken an ember jewel from Zeus that will give him access to the castle," Leon says, standing.

212

"Please tell me you're joking," Pem says.

"I wish I was," Kaly says.

Avi's infinity charm warms against her chest. She reaches up and presses her hand against it. "I think Pemphredo is reaching out."

"Where's Deino and Enyo?" Xena asks.

Pem points up to the window. "They helped Dita and Andromeda take Perseus up to a suite."

"Perseus is back?" Itra asks.

"Dita showed up at the window right after Chronos was shoved into the helix," Avi says, pulling out her necklace. "Perseus looked half dead."

Leon sighs. "We've searched the grounds here." He points to Avi. "Reach out to the sisters. Maybe one of them saw something or picked it up." He releases his staff and throws up a light stone.

"Enyo," Avi says. *"We have a situation. Where are you?"*

"In the present cavern," Enyo says. *"Meet us in the dining hall."*

"Ok," Avi says. "Ember, dining hall, please."

Itra and Leon appear inside the dining hall simultaneously.

Zana squeals and rushes towards Leon. "Catch!"

Leon steps back and catches her. "Zana!"

Zana wraps her arms around his neck.

"Oh, side note," Itra whispers. "I'm sure you noticed Ora managed to rewind time."

Leon squeezes Zana a little closer. He looks over her shoulder. "Where are the others?"

Danae walks over to Itra and Leon.

Itra turns in a slow circle. "Danae, did you see the ladies before we arrived?"

"No, why?" Danae asks, looping her arm through his.

"Avi had Ember bring us here."

"*Kaly,*" Leon says.

"*Leon!*" Kaly shrills. "*He's back! He's in the present cavern!*"

"*Chronos?*" Leon gently sets Zana down. "I'm going to check on your mom. Be right back." He bolts for the conservatory door, but Itra grabs his arm.

"What's on fire?" Itra asks.

Leon shakes off his grip. "Follow or stay." He looks over at Danae. "Stay in here." Danae frowns and salutes Leon.

Leon winks at Zana and then takes a right into the conservatory.

Itra follows close on his heels.

Anton wanders over to Danae. "Any idea what that was about?"

"Guessing it is the absence of Kaly."

Anton tugs on his collar. "Trouble?"

"Let's hope not," Danae says, taking Zana's hand. "Who's hungry?"

"Me!" Emit yells, yanking out a chair and plopping down.

A large plate of nachos appears before Danae gets to the table. She laughs.

"Ever the patient young man," Danae says, helping Zana into a chair.

Ora slides into a chair beside Emit.

Elis points up at the dome. "Any idea what time it is?"

"After sunset," Anton says, inspecting the darkness shadowing the glass panels.

"Didn't we just get here?" Emit asks, over a full mouth.

"Emit," Danae says, glaring at him.

He swallows and wipes his mouth with his sleeve. "Sorry mom, but we just got here." He points to Elis. "We left first thing in the morning, right?"

Elis nods, scooping up a chip. "Before dawn."

"Check your watch," Ora says, pointing to Anton.

Anton pats his pants, pulls out his pocket watch, and pops it open. "That can't be right." He turns the face of the clock with the date visible towards Danae. "We arrived on Tuesday."

Danae whispers, "It's been two days."

Anton snaps the watch closed. "Danae, a word in the library, please?"

Danae swallows a chip and follows Anton to the library.

Anton whirls when they cross the threshold and points his finger a hair away from Danae's nose.

"Whoa," Danae says and takes a step back.

Anton drops his hand and sighs. "I keep getting a sense of forgetting something. And now this time jump or whatever the hell you're not telling me. My anxiety is quickly escalating."

Danae raises her hands. "Just take a breath." She glances at the kids around the table. "We arrived here two days ago. That's true."

Anton takes a step back bumping against a bookshelf.

"Ora can turn back time," Danae says softly. "The memories of what happened were wiped to save them from the trauma."

"Trauma?" Anton glances out at the table.

"Give me your hand," Danae says.

Anton hesitantly sets his hand in her awaiting palm.

"This will be hard to see," Danae says. "Are you ready?"

Anton swallows and nods.

She places her thumb with the gold ring on his hand.

Anton wobbles and shakes his head. A flash of the chaotic vacant war room, the open panel in the dome, Ana lying lifeless on the ground, and Elis's face in the mirror stuck in the City of Time. "No!" He closes his eyes, and a single tear falls down his cheek.

"Are you ok?" Danae asks.

Anton sighs. "I don't know..." He sniffles. "Is it even safe here?"

"Great question," Danae says. "Teuta!"

Teuta appears next to Danae. "Here."

Danae glares at Teuta's loose ponytail and rosy cheeks; and takes special note that her top is on backwards and inside out.

Anton coughs to cover his laugh.

Teuta blanches. "What did I miss?"

Danae raises an eyebrow. "I take it Junior's health has returned?"

Teuta takes note of her clothing for the first time and her wardrobe changes in less than a blink. "He's much better. Where are the others?"

"Why are you asking me?" Danae asks, pointing down at her petite frame. "If you weren't making up for lost time with a certain arrogant giant, you'd notice that something is not quite right. What's happened with the weather? Or is night again?""

Teuta flares her nose and vanishes.

"I feel a new presence here." Danae mentally counts the number of souls in the castle. Twice. "There is one too many." She turns to Anton. "I need to get you and the kids somewhere safe. No arguments."

She walks out of the library and over to the table where the kids are eating. "How about we take this food to go?" A door appears beside her. She opens the door and inspects the space. "In you go."

Anton hesitates, but Elis takes Zana's hand. He nods to Danae as they step through.

Emit and Ora follow Zana.

Anton takes a step in and turns to Danae. "Are you following?"

She shakes her head. "I'll be there soon. Lock the door and don't answer for anyone."

"Danae..."

"I said no arguments," Danae says, pushing Anton inside. She closes the door, and it vanishes. *Itra, where are you guys?*

45

Thunder clammers overhead.

Itra ducks in response. *"Danae, I'm in the maze with Leon. Are you and the kids safe?"*

"I sent Anton and the kids to our house," Danae says, running through the conservatory towards the front entrance.

Danae takes the steps up two at a time and slides to a stop at the landing window overlooking the maze.

Itra turns to the window. *"Stay out of sight."* He points up. *"It's Perendi, and he's mad as hell."*

Danae spots the outline of a man in the dark clouds. *"Why are you out in the open? Are you guys trying to get killed?"* She glances at the singed hedges.

Leon looks over his shoulder and finds Danae at the window. *"He's trying to break into the vault by blowing up the fairy statue."*

"Teuta!" Danae screams.

Teuta appears next to Danae.

"Can't you 'tani' him to hell?" Danae says, pointing up at the clouds.

"Tani," Teuta says.

Danae vanishes and lands on a soft, bouncy surface. *No, she didn't!*

"Who's there?" Anton asks from outside Danae's bedroom door.

"Worthless damn fairy." Danae opens the door. "She sent me home instead of sending Perendi away!"

Anton frowns. "He's is at the castle?"

"Yes, are you and the kids good here?"

"They're good," Anton says, pointing a thumb over his shoulder. "They're in the kitchen raiding the fridge."

"Good," Danae says. "I need to go back. Can you stay?"

Anton laughs. "Zero cars to take me anywhere else..."

Danae shakes her head. "That's right. I'm so sorry."

"Don't be," Anton says, holding up his gold bracelet. "I'll call if we need anything."

"Thank you," Danae says. "Be back soon."

A door appears to her right.

"Stay safe," Anton says, as she steps through and vanishes.

Danae returns to the landing and edges closer to the window.

A thick layer of smoke hangs over the hedge maze.

"Itra, Leon!" She balls her fists and pounds on the glass. *Where are they?* She closes her eyes and concentrates. She feels at least three people up one floor. She ascends the steps and starts jogging down the rounded stone corridor. "Dita! Are you still here?"

Dita pokes her head out of a door a few paces ahead. "Danae?"

"Oh," Danae says breathlessly. "Thank God. Where is everyone?"

"Andromeda and Perseus are here. I haven't seen Enyo and Deino for a while. They helped me get him to bed." She gestures to Perseus, restlessly fidgeting on the bed, with Andromeda curled up next to him.

"Do you know what was wrong with him?"

"He was dehydrated. I've given him a dose of lavender powder to help him relax a bit and allow some time for the

218

fluids to replenish him." She points to the drip bags hanging on the bedpost above his head.

"Odd," Danae says, shaking her head. "Junior improved well enough to take Teuta to bed."

"Junior was ill?" Dita asks, looking out the door.

"He stumbled into the dining hall and passed out just before they tossed Chronos from the castle. He had a weak pulse but was breathing on his own."

"Where is he?"

"I'm guessing still in Teuta's bed."

Dita snorts. "A lifetime of frustration realized."

Perseus groans.

Danae steps back out into the corridor. "I need to find the others."

"I'll try to get Junior," Dita says, nodding to Danae.

"Teuta," Danae calls, jogging down the corridor towards the landing between floors. *"Itra, Leon, Kaly!"*

"Danae!" Kaly answers. *"Are the kids safe?"*

"Yes, where are you?" Danae pauses on the landing. *Up or down, why isn't this damn gift working?*

"We're stuck in between the present and future cavern."

"Down it is," Danae says, running down to the first floor. *"On my way."* She makes a sharp left at the bottom and descends the spiral steps across from the conservatory.

About three turns in she feels someone behind her. She whirls, raising her fists to swing. The motion throws her off balance. She wobbles on the edge of the step but can't right herself. She falls hard, nailing her tailbone, somersaulting over, and crashing into the curve of the stairwell.

"Oh no, no, no!" A figure races down the steps. He calls his staff and hovers the ember light over her crumpled form. "Danae, are you ok?"

"Can't breathe," Danae wheezes, inspecting his face. "Noel?"

Noel nods and frowns. "I didn't mean to startle you."

"When did you get here?" Danae asks, attempting to sit up. She winces and applies pressure to her side.

"Five minutes ago," Noel says, kneeling beside her. "Teuta appeared in my house, ranting about the others being trapped and my duty to serve." He offers her a hand.

Danae shakes her head. "I don't think I can move at the moment." She leans to her right taking pressure off her backside. "Go help the others. Kaly said they were trapped between the present and future caverns."

"Do you know who trapped them there?" Noel asks, looking down the steps.

"Not a hundred percent sure." Danae feels the back of her head. "We've fought off Chronos, but Perendi was back trying to break into the vault. My guess is Perendi? Or—hell, maybe the devil himself at this point. Be careful."

"I can't just leave you here," Noel says.

"Dita's here," Danae says, pointing up. "I'll be fine. Just go."

Noel taps his head. "Shout if you're not!"

Danae nods.

〽

Noel makes his way down the steps with quiet precision. He slows his pace when he rounds the curve near the large. closed wood and iron door. He silently maneuvers to the door, lowers to a push up, and looks under. He spots three pairs of shoes— boots much like his own, gold winged sandals, and blue tennis shoes. *Three men—possibly Leon, Hermes, and Itra.* He pushes up to stand but pauses and lowers back to the ground.

A shadow crosses over the ground just in front of the boots. *Four.*

"Leon!" Noel says. *"Move your foot once if you can hear me."*

"Noel?"

"Good you can talk," Noel says. *"Need a little help in there?"*

"Perendi has trapped Kaly, Xena, Pem, Enyo, and Deino in the passage between the past and future cavern."

"Are they hurt?"

"No, but don't freak out—he's using Avi as a shield."

220

"Fuck!" Noel pushes back up and skips up a few steps until he is concealed around the curve.

He whispers, "Open says me."

The large door swings open.

Noel remains glued to the wall and out of sight.

"Who dares to interrupt me?" Perendi yells, glancing at the open door.

"Noel," Leon says, *"stay out of sight! He throws lightning."*

"Ember," a female voice sings.

The last syllable echoes around the cavern and up the stairs.

"He's starting to sweat," Leon says.

"The second you see a chance to get Avi," Noel says, *"don't hesitate."*

"Perendi," Ember says, "you've trespassed. Leave now breathing or dead like your wife."

Perendi tightens his arm around Avi's chest. "Don't you dare speak of my wife!" He points to Hermes. "Her murderer is standing in this very room."

Leon moves an inch in front of Hermes. Perendi scowls at Leon.

Leon double taps his staff to the glowing scythe and stares Perendi down.

"Your wife died," Ember says. "That's true. But your blood feud right ended when you killed Mui."

Perendi looks around the cavern. "That's not justice."

"Leave or die," Ember whispers in Perendi's ear.

Perendi turns, dropping his arm from around Avi.

Avi lunges away from him and Leon pounces.

Perendi turns back and raises his arm to block Leon's swinging scythe.

Hermes rushes forward and pushes Avi towards the door.

Noel releases his staff and leaps down the steps.

"Don't hurt me!" Avi shouts, covering her head and face with her arms.

"It's me," Noel whispers. "I've got you." He tugs on one of her arms.

Avi cowers back.

Noel lowers his face level with hers. "Babe, look at me."

"Noel?" Avi drops her arms and looks up.

He smiles and nods.

A lightning bolt ricochets off the cavern walls.

Hermes and Itra duck behind one of the large stalagmites.

Avi yelps and jumps into Noel's arms. He carries her up the steps and around the first curve. "I'm going to help Leon."

"Wait," Avi says, gripping her infinity charm.

Enyo and Deino appear on either side of Perendi.

Enyo winks at Leon raising her sword. *"We aren't really here."*

"What the..." Perendi stammers.

Noel quickly kisses Avi and silently slinks down the steps. He calls his staff and taps once. The ember glow flares to life. He lowers the light to the ground.

"Let's make him burn," Noel says, edging his way into the cavern.

Perendi raises his hand. Static pops and a buzz of electricity hums. Another bolt forms in his hand.

The ground starts to shake.

Leon fakes left, fades right, and then spots Noel. He taps his staff to the ember glow and follows Noel's lead, lowering his flare to the ground. A circle of fire ignites around Perendi.

Enyo and Deino step back and the four of them surround him.

Perendi throws the lightning bolt. It bounces off the wall of fire. He ducks, but the bolt strikes his right shoulder.

Enyo laughs.

Hermes and Itra stand.

"Not so fun, is it?" Junior asks from the threshold. "You killed my father." He saunters into the cavern. "Today I get the pleasure of watching you burn."

Hermes and Itra join Junior.

"Ember!" Perendi shouts.

"You had a choice," Ember sings.

The fire closes in around him. "Wait! I choose to live."

Leon and Noel look at Junior.

222

"Had a choice," Junior says, shaking his head.

The flames engulf him in an instant.

Teuta appears next to Junior. She takes Junior's hand. "He's gone."

Junior nods.

"Tani," Teuta says.

The fire and the remains of Perendi disappear.

Itra sighs. "Where the hell were you two when we called?"

"I was getting Noel," Teuta says, pointing at Leon's doppelgänger.

Avi hesitantly steps into the cavern. She takes Noel's hand. "Can we please free the ladies now?" She points to the large boulder blocking the passage to the future cavern.

Teuta raises her hand. The boulder shakes and then crumbles—the dust blast blinds everyone.

Leon covers his face. "Kaly?"

"Here," Kaly coughs, helping Xena over the rocks.

"Pem," Xena says.

"Right behind you." Pem steps beside Xena. "Deino and Enyo are good. We're all fine."

Leon checks Kaly over.

"We need to check on Danae and the kids," Kaly says, hugging Leon.

"Um, Danae fell hard on the steps," Noel says.

Itra sprints towards the door but it slams shut in his face. He whirls and marches over to Teuta.

"My sister was taking care of her when I came down," Junior says, stepping between Teuta and Itra.

"Then let me check on her," Itra says. He attempts to push Junior aside and fails.

Leon calls his staff and double taps. "Open the damn door, Teuta." He steps beside Itra.

"I didn't close it," Teuta says, folding her arms across her chest.

"Ember," Leon says, "so help me—if you harm my sister..."

"Danae and Dita are fine," Junior says. "Put your weapons down." He glares at Leon's scythe and Enyo's hand gripping the hilt of her sword. "We are here to protect and serve Ember and the Castle of Teskom."

"And that's what we've been doing," Enyo says. "Unlike you." She points to Junior. "You failed to be part of the action."

Junior glances at Teuta. "My absence was not for nothing. I had to visit the City of Time."

Teuta nods. "Ora lived in the City of Time for thirty years. We had to notify her spouse that she would not be returning."

"She was married?" Itra asks.

Teuta nods. "And she had two children."

Itra steps forward, then teeters back and collapses.

Leon breaks his fall, and Hermes gently lowers him to the ground.

Leon spots an ember jewel dangling from a gold chain around Hermes's neck.

"Was that your fathers?" Leon asks, pointing to Hermes as he tucks the jewel back under his tunic.

"Yes," Hermes says. "He gave it to me just before he stepped into the hedge maze."

"Oh, thank goodness," Kaly says. "We thought he lost it during his confrontation with Chronos."

"Oh!" Teuta yelps. "That would have been really bad."

Leon looks up at Teuta. "Back to what made my brother-in-law pass out. Are you saying my niece is a mother?"

Teuta nods once.

Sunlight dances in from the window across from Danae. She stirs.

Itra stands from the corner chair and sits on the edge of the bed. "Good morning."

Danae opens an eye. "Morning?"

Itra nods towards the window. "Just barely."

She attempts to sit up and groans. "We're still inside the castle," she says, looking around. "What did I miss?"

"Perendi came back for revenge, but Junior got his."

Danae frowns. "Was anyone hurt?"

"Just Perendi," Itra says, "and you."

"That was really just a clumsy accident," Danae says. "Is Noel still here?"

Itra laughs. "I'm pretty sure he and Avi haven't left their suite."

"Really?" Danae inches up with Itra's help.

"Pem even mentioned a wedding."

Danae adjusts one of the pillows. "Something to celebrate and not fear is a welcome idea."

"I checked in with Anton," Itra says, holding up his wrist with the gold bracelet. "They're doing fine. Eating everything in the fridge. He had to order a pizza last night."

Danae chuckles and grimaces. "I thought Dita would have healed my ribs."

"She gave you something for the pain while she set them. One was broken, grazing your lung and three were fractured. Plus, you busted your tailbone. You're going to be sore for a bit."

"All that damage from a few steps?" Danae asks.

"Noel described it as a total wipeout."

"Knock, knock," Dita says from the door.

"Good morning," Itra says, moving away from the bed.

"It's a great morning." Dita moves to Danae's side. "How's the pain?"

"A solid seven out of ten."

"No running or lifting for a few weeks," Dita says, tightening the compression wrap around Danae's chest. "Your ribs are healing with Ember's help, but they are not yet healed."

"Got it," Danae says, nodding to the door. "Is Perseus awake yet?"

"He is," Dita says. "And he's nearly recovered."

Dita glances at Itra. He shakes his head.

"I'll leave you two alone," Dita says. "The family has asked for a meeting in the dining hall in a bit. Come on down when you're ready."

Dita closes the door.

Danae glares at Itra, who is pacing the length of the bed. "What happened?"

Itra pauses and comes to her side. He sits but then stands.

"Just spill it." Danae frowns. "You're obviously too anxious to sit still."

"While you were sleeping, we saw the playback of the kids in the City of Time." Danae nods and Itra continues. "After Zeus absorbed the urtar stone in the chamber where Princess Danae was held. Ora couldn't pass through the ember archway or portal to the communist dimension with the others."

Danae holds a hand over her chest. "Right."

Itra nods. "The only place she could go was back to the City of Time." He takes Danae's hands and takes a deep breath. "She made a life there. She had a husband and two children—a family."

Danae lets out a choked sob. "No!"

Itra's bottom lip quivers. "Technically, we're grandparents."

"But now she's seven again," Danae says.

"She left them to save us," Itra says. "Pemphredo was sharing this news with Deino and Enyo via the present cavern when Perendi ambushed them."

Danae catches a few falling tears with the heel of her hand. "The kids had lives, families..."

"And they will again," Itra says, wrapping her in a gentle hug.

Itra holds the door open for Danae.

She steps into the dining hall.

A halo of light hangs over the table. The murmur of conversation quiets.

Kaly rounds the table. "Danae, are you ok?"

"I've had better days," Danae whispers, hugging Kaly. "I'm sore physically and gut punched emotionally."

Kaly leans back and nods. "I understand." She smiles at her hovering husband.

"Hey bro," Danae says, turning to face him. "You good?"

"Better than you," Leon says. "How're the ribs?"

"Tender."

"Danae, I'm really sorry," Noel says, walking up to them.

"Really," Danae says, "it's not your fault."

Teuta flutters around the group. "Ember is waiting. Please take your seats."

Itra pulls out a chair for Danae and he takes the chair next to her.

Danae nods to Dita, Xena, and Pem across the table. Noel sits next to Avi. Kaly and Leon take their seats across from Enyo.

"Where's Deino, Andromeda, Perseus, and Hermes?" Danae whispers to Kaly.

"They returned to the City of Time about ten minutes ago to prepare for Zeus's funeral."

Danae nods.

Junior and Teuta sit on opposite ends of the table.

"Today we celebrate the service of our fellow descendants," Teuta says, raising a glass of wine.

Similar glasses appear in front of each person.

"It's a little early for wine," Xena mutters, lifting her glass.

"Gezuar!" Itra says.

The descendants respond in unison. "Gezuar!"

Teuta takes a sip and continues. "And Ember has recognized the engagement of Avi and Noel."

Pem squeals and claps. "I knew it!"

A round of applause and a few whistles echo in the hall.

Avi extends her hand for Kaly and Danae to see her new ring, a large round diamond set between two ember stones on a white gold band.

"It's stunning," Danae says. "I'm so happy for you!"

Avi blushes. "Thank you!"

"Did you decide where you will reside?" Pem asks.

Avi glances at Teuta.

Teuta nods.

"Ember has given us her blessing to reside in the revolutionary dimension, but we'll have access to the Ottoman dimension to visit his family."

"That's wonderful," Xena says.

"Thank you," Avi says. "Ember has also acknowledged another union." She glances at Junior.

Leon drums his hands on the edge of the table.

Dita laughs. "It's about time."

Teuta stands and transforms from her fairy height to her regal, queenly self.

Leon stops the drumroll.

"Yes. It's true. Junior and I are going to be residing here together as the messengers for Ember."

"Does that mean Junior will have a fairy form too?" Leon asks.

Noel laughs and the others join in with a snicker. A snort and a full belly laugh comes from Xena.

Junior glares at Leon.

Enyo raises her glass to Junior and grins. "Congratulations!"

The table shares another clink of glasses.

"Well done brother," Dita says, tipping her glass towards him.

Junior tips his glass to her with a cheeky grin.

"Ember honors the sacrifice that Ora made in, leaving her family and defeating Chronos," Teuta says. "Her children are well provided for and are watched over by Princess Danae."

Danae takes Itra's hand and squeezes once. "Thank you, sincerely, that news is comforting."

"Ora's memories... will they ever come back?" Itra asks.

"Her subconscious may have flashes of a previous life," Teuta says, "but she and the other children will have no memories of the castle, their experiences here, or the thirty years they experienced."

Itra nods and squeezes Danae's hand. "And Vincent?"

"He's alive and well," Teuta says.

"Good," Itra says.

"Are we clear of any looming threats?" Danae asks.

Teuta nods. "My only visit in the near future will be to deliver an invitation to a wedding." She winks at Avi.

"I couldn't imagine having the ceremony without all of you," Avi says.

Noel nods. "And I've already asked Leon to be my best man."

Pem pouts.

Avi laughs. "And I was going to ask Pem to be my maid of honor."

"Really?" Pem says, smiling.

"Of course!" Avi says. "And Zana and Ora as the flower girls?"

Kaly and Danae answer in unison. "Yes!"

"Then yes," Teuta says. "Your next adventure here will be for a celebration." She winks at Junior. "Tani!"

Junior smiles at Teuta from across the table. "And now there's only two. What shall we do?"

47

Ora runs from the mailbox to the front porch. "Mom!"

"In the kitchen," Danae says, taking a batch of snickerdoodle cookies out of the oven.

"We've got mail," Ora says, holding up a square purple envelope. "My name is on this one. Can I open it?"

Danae glances at the envelope as she transfers a cookie from the pan to a plate. The cookie slides off the spatula onto the counter.

"Mom, you dropped the cookie!"

Danae sets the spatula down and reaches for the envelope.

Ora rolls her eyes and gives up the mail. She charges past Danae and takes the remaining cookies off the pan. Making sure Danae isn't watching, she helps herself to the broken cookie on the counter.

Danae examines the names: Itra, Danae, Emit and Ora. Their names are written in elegant, gold cursive.

Ora sighs. "Mom, can I please open it?"

"Yes, but after dinner. I want your dad and brother to be here since it's addressed to all of us."

"Fine," Ora says.

"Dinner is in thirty minutes," Danae says, setting the mail on top of the fridge. She goes back to scooping out the cookie dough onto the pan and then places it back in the oven. She restarts the timer on her phone. It vibrates with a notification and then a second.

Danae opens the first message from Kaly. *We got mail. Did you?*

"Hmm." She closes Kaly's message and opens one from Anton. *I received an envelope today addressed to Elis and "his father, Anton." Did the kids send something to Elis?*

Danae glances at the fridge. She texts them back in a group message. *It appears all of us received mail today. We'll open ours after dinner. Group chat?*

Danae drums her fingernails on the countertop waiting for a response.

"Do I smell snickerdoodles?" Itra says, sniffing his way into the kitchen.

Danae laughs. "Of course. Dinner's almost ready." She points to the crock pot. "Did you hear from Uncle Vincent today?" She swats his hand away from the plate of cookies.

Itra frowns. "No, but I haven't had my phone on me. I'll go check if you let me have a cookie?"

"Not happening, mister." She kisses his nose then swats his behind. "Go check."

Her phone shakes against the counter. *Timer or message?* She swipes her screen and taps the timer. *Two minutes left.* She opens the group message.

Kaly response, *Give us two hours. Zana is at play rehearsal.*

Danae types back. *Sounds good, Anton?*

He types back one word. *Sure.*

Emit wipes his mouth and gathers his plate and utensils. "Elis called and said we have a family meeting. Do you know what it will be about?" He stands and pushes in his chair.

Danae nods. "We've received some mail today. I've asked Anton and Kaly to call us in about an hour."

Ora frowns. "You said we'd open it after dinner."

"Sorry," Danae says, handing Emit her plate. "Zana is at play rehearsal for another hour."

Itra wipes the remaining juice from his plate with the last of the bread before handing it to Emit. "Uncle Vincent said he would walk Duke and check his mailbox," he checks his watch, "about now."

Ora pushes back from the table with her plate and follows Emit to the sink.

Itra takes a cookie and smells it. "It's like a little taste of Christmas in one bite." He shoves the entire cookie into his mouth.

"So much for savoring it." Danae pushes back from the table and sighs. "Do you think it's good news?"

"Maybe," Itra says, nibbling another cookie. He jumps up.

Danae startles holding her hand to her chest. "What's wrong?"

"I left the sprinkler on." He puts his phone on the table. "Answer it if Uncle Vincent calls back."

Honk honk

Itra slides on his boots and shields his eyes from the setting sun. He recognizes Ermal's patrol car.

"Coming!" Itra jogs down the drive and opens the gate.

Ermal waves and drives through.

Itra slides the gate closed and jogs back up the drive. He holds up a finger. "One second, I've got to turn off the sprinkler."

Ermal nods and steps out of his cruiser.

Danae pokes her head out the front door. "Hey Ermal. Have you eaten? I can make you a plate."

"Hi Danae." Ermal says, holding up a purple envelope.

"Oh," Danae says. "We haven't opened ours yet. Come on in."

"Sprinkler's off." Itra slides off his boots and pats Ermal on the shoulder. "What's up?"

Ermal shows Itra the envelope.

"Ah, I see." Itra follows Ermal inside.

"Ermal!" Ora says, tossing the dish towel at Emit. She runs over to Ermal. They fist bump twice, slap hands three times, snap once, and wink.

Ermal laughs. "Nailed it!"

Emit stacks the last plate on the rack. "You two are the biggest dorks imaginable."

"You're just jealous you don't have a secret handshake with Ermal."

"Dork is better than other names I've been called today," Ermal says, patting the handcuffs on his belt.

"Busy day?" Danae asks, setting a plate of dinner on the table.

"Arrested two kids for shoplifting and vandalism." Ermal takes a seat. "Thanks Danae."

Itra lifts the whiskey bottle. "Are you still on duty?"

"Unfortunately, yes," Ermal says.

"Coffee it is," Danae says, filling up the kettle. "Hot chocolate for the big kids?"

"Yes, please!" Itra says.

Danae rolls her eyes at Itra. He plants a kiss on her cheeks.

Emit sees the kiss and makes a gagging sound before marching out of the kitchen.

Ermal sets the purple envelope on the table.

"You got one too?" Ora asks, inspecting the envelope. She turns it over. "Mom, he opened his."

"And we'll open ours with the others. Patience my dear."

Ermal winks at Ora and whispers, "It's good news."

"Really?" Ora whispers.

Ermal nods and takes a bite of bread.

"Emit, can you check the pantry for marshmallows?" Danae asks.

"That's a negative," Emit says, from the other room.

"Are you sure?" Danae says, stirring in the mixtures of cocoa and steaming milk. "I just bought two bags."

Emit walks back into the kitchen. "Dad, do you want to rat on yourself, or should I?"

Itra turns towards Danae and bats his eyes. "Mercy darlin."

"Itra!" Danae swats a dish towel at him. He dodges the assault and opens a plastic container on the other end of the counter.

"But we did make rice crispy treats."

One small, sticky square is left inside.

"We?" Danae turns to Ora.

"It wasn't me," Ora says, holding up her hands. She points one finger at Emit.

"I see," Danae says. "Hot cocoa and no marshmallows for the boys." She pulls out a stash of marshmallows from her baking supplies and sprinkles five on top of two mugs. "Ermal, would you like a few with your coffee?"

Itra and Emit stick out their bottom lips and cock their heads to the same side simultaneously.

"Sure." Ermal hides his grin behind a napkin.

Ora laughs and takes the mug from Danae. She sits next to Ermal.

Emit and Itra take their mugs and sit in the chairs across from them, sulking.

When Ermal finishes eating. Danae replaces his plate with his marshmallow-topped coffee. "Ora, please dial Anton and Kaly in the group chat. Itra, see if you can get Uncle Vincent on your phone." She washes and rinses the plate and sticks it in the drying rack.

Kaly answers on the first ring. "Hey, Leon and Zana are in the driveway, one second."

Anton's face fills part of the screen a few seconds later. "Sorry had a last-minute board meeting. Hey, is that Ermal?"

Ora sets the phone up on the corner of the table.

Ermal waves at the camera. "Hey Anton, how's it going?"

"Good, thanks." Anton leans back in his chair. "Elis, get in here, please."

"We're here!" Kaly says, returning to the video chat with Zana and Leon.

"Hey Ermal!" Leon says, leaning closer to the phone. His nose fills the screen.

"Lean, back up," Kaly says, tugging on Leon's shoulder. "Your face is blocking the screen."

Ora giggles.

Elis leans over Anton's shoulder. "What's all this about?"

"Hold on," Itra says, setting up his phone with Uncle Vincent on the other side of the table.

Duke barks. "Settle down Duke," says Uncle Vincent.

Danae hands Ora the envelope from the top of the fridge. "Let's open our messages."

Zana takes the envelope from Kaly. She peels it open and slides out a gold and purple edged card.

"Oh, pretty," Zana and Ora say in unison.

"What is it?" Itra asks.

"We're cordially invited to the wedding of Mui Junior and Teuta this Friday," Ora says.

"Flip it over," Zana says.

"And Avi and Noel's wedding on Saturday," Ora says. "Who are they?"

"Where is the Castle of Teskom?" Elis asks, reading over Anton's shoulder.

"They are old friends of the family, and the castle is close by," Danae answers. Then she turns to wink at Vincent. "Are you able to make the trip?"

Vincent smiles. "Absolutely." He holds up his thumb with a gold ring.

"Anton?" Danae asks.

"I'll check the calendar," Anton says. "Friday may be a challenge on such short notice, but I can send Elis. School gets out midday on Friday." He pulls at his buttoned collar. "I know the names sound familiar, but I can't place a face. Are they related somehow?"

Itra nods. "Actually, very distant relatives."

"I'm invited as a plus one," Ermal says, tapping his envelope. "But whose?"

Danae and Itra laugh.

"What did you two do?" Kaly asks.

Itra shakes his head. "It wasn't us."

"You're welcome," Leon says.

Ermal frowns. "Are you setting me up with some broad?"

Leon laughs. "You could say that you've fancied her for centuries."

Ermal rolls his eyes and checks his phone. "I've got to go." He points to Leon. "But you are getting a phone call later to explain whatever this is about."

Leon smirks and salutes. "Talk soon."

"Leave the gate open," Itra says to Ermal. "I'll take care of it after the call."

"I know you're in on this," Ermal says, tapping the envelope on Itra's head.

"It must be a sunset wedding," Danae says, looking over the details. "Do you want to get ready here or in the suites at the castle?"

Kaly looks at Leon.

"We can go straight there," Leon says. "There's more space and it has a better wardrobe."

"Castle it is," Kaly says, winking at Danae. "Xena texted about an hour ago. She and Pem are arriving on Thursday. See you Friday around three?"

Itra nods. "We'll pick up Elis and Vincent."

"I don't need to be picked up," Vincent says, holding up his thumb again.

"That's right," Danae says. "Anton, let us know if you're free."

"Will do," Anton says. "Good night."

They respond in unison. "Good night."

The calls disconnect.

"Do I have to go?" Emit says. "Weddings are sappy and boring."

"You can keep Uncle Vincent company," Danae says. "He's likely to feel the same."

"Do we get to go shopping?" Ora says, bouncing up and down in the chair.

"Actually," Danae says, "Teuta and Avi would like you and Zana to be the flower girls for their ceremonies."

"Really?" Ora grins.

"And the dresses will be perfect," Danae says.

"Dresses?" Ora asks, holding up two fingers. "There are two?"

"Yes," Danae says.

Ora races around the table and throws her arms around Danae. "Thank you, thank you, thank you!"

48

Ora and Zana twirl in their purple dresses. The layers of red tulle flutter out.

"We've only been here five minutes and they're already twirling," Kaly says.

"I wish we had some way to capture the moment," Danae says.

"According to Teuta," Avi says. "We can play back anything that happens here in the castle with a thought, and it will display on command."

"Anything?" Danae blushes, trying to keep her thoughts away from her first shower with Itra.

Kaly elbows Danae's side. "Why are your cheeks on fire?"

Danae coughs. "It's kind of hot in here, right?"

Avi and Kaly laugh.

Ora collapses to the ground. "I'm so dizzy."

"Alright," Danae says, helping her up. "Let's try on the gold and blue dress for Teuta's ceremony."

Their dresses transform in an instant. The layers of tulle are replaced with silk chiffon. The tiered ruffles of royal blue lead up to an empire waist and a gold top.

"Oh wow," Danae says, standing back to look them over. "That's a stunning color on both of you."

Zana slides her hand over the skirt. "It's so soft!"

"I love them both!" Ora says, turning to the mirror.

"Good," Danae says, "they're beautiful. And now for your hair. What do you think?"

Ora and Zana stand shoulder to shoulder in front of the mirror.

Teuta appears behind them in her fairy form wearing a silk robe.

Ora and Zana jump and turn. "Teuta!" Their memories of the castle and Ember had come back the instant they arrived, through the details of their last visit did not.

"These dresses deserve a tiara," Teuta says, turning them back towards the mirror.

Their hair is instantly pulled up into two fancy updos with a few ringlets falling around their faces. Perched on top are shiny gold and sapphire encrusted tiara.

"Oh my goodness," Zana says, reaching up to touch the tiara.

"Wow," Kaly says. "Our little princesses."

Danae wipes away a falling tear.

"Mom, are you crying?" Ora says, studying Danae in the mirror.

"You two look so beautiful."

"Emit's right," Ora whispers to Zana. "Weddings are sappy. Thank you Teuta. When do we get to see your dress?"

Teuta transforms to her full height. Her dark auburn ponytail mirrors the girls updo style and is topped with a gold tiara that has a single enormous sapphire in the center. The robe transforms into a shimmery cream gown made of silk. It has an empire waist and fine blue and gold threaded embellishments across the top. Layers of tulle under the skirt add volume.

Teuta gives them a small curtsy.

"You look absolutely stunning," Danae says.

"Junior is going to lose his mind!" Kaly says.

"Give us a twirl!" Zana claps.

Teuta turns in a slow circle. The back of the gown drapes low, with more blue and gold details along the train.

"Wow," Ora says. "You're a true queen!"

Knock, knock

"Ladies, five minutes," Itra says from the corridor.

"On our way," Danae says.

238

"What are you two going to wear?" Ora asks Danae and Kaly.

Danae and Kaly twirl, transforming their jeans and sweaters into full ball gowns.

"Magic!" Zana whispers.

Danae and Kaly stand shoulder to shoulder in the mirror.

Kaly skims her hands over the fitted emerald bodice. "I think this color matches your eyes, Zana." She twists side to side and the voluminous skirt swishes the floor.

Zana inches closer to the mirror. "You're right!"

Danae looks down at her gown in the mirror. "What do you think, red or burgundy?" The gown transforms, and the silk organza splits into half red, half burgundy.

"Red!" Ora says clapping. "Dad's not ready for all this!" She waves her hand from Danae's curly cropped pixie cut down the length of her dress.

"Well, let's go knock all the men's socks off." Kaly holds the door open to the corridor.

The guests stand in the spaces of the parapet facing west. The sun dances across the lake to the mountains of Montenegro.

Junior takes his spot, aligning his large frame with the sun.

Teuta appears on the opposite side. She bows her head and looks over at Junior. He dips his chin in return.

An iridescent bridge appears between them, crossing over the hedge maze far below.

A cellist plucks the first few notes of a swaying melody.

Ora and Zana step in front of Teuta and up onto the bridge in time with the music.

Ora looks straight ahead. Zana peers down and sways. Ora adjusts the basket over her wrist and takes Zana's hand. She whispers, "Eyes up."

Zana nods and draws her attention back to the horizon.

They walk, dropping red rose petals across the bridge over to Junior's side.

The melody dips an octave lower and slows to half time.

Teuta steps onto the bridge with her eyes fixed on Junior.

"I knew she did drama well," Danae says, nudging Itra. "But this is next level."

Itra nods. "All I keep seeing are dollar signs for Ora's future wedding budget. Nothing will top this."

"Oh, but if Ember carries the cost like this, we're covered!"

"Ha!" Itra nudges Danae. "Look at Enyo and Ermal."

"Oh, he is head over heals in lust for that woman!" Danae says, nodding to Leon and glancing in Ermal's direction.

Leon smirks. He whispers something to Kaly.

Kaly spots Ermal's gaze lingering over Enyo. She snickers and then clamps her hand over her mouth. She meets Danae's eyes and turns away to silence her laughter.

The music slows and fades as Junior takes Teuta's hand.

The sun levels between the couple just before they are announced husband and wife. Their kiss signals the cellist to play once again. They pull away to the roar of applause, whistles, and shouts.

Teuta turns to the descendants and bows. "It's my honor to serve Ember and the Castle of Teskom." She takes her hand wrapped in Junior's and raises their arms. "To protect and serve."

Champagne flutes appear in everyone's hands. They lift their glasses and chant in unison. "To protect and serve."

Acknowledgements

The Ember in Time Series is only possible because of my dearest love and partner for life, Art. He gave me the creative space and time to release the story whirling around in my head. His support means more than I can express. I hope that my readers have or have had a partner in life that can hold or have held the torch to light your path as you pursue or have pursued your passion and cheer them on.

And to my faithful editor, Jenny Leonard, and my beta readers. Your feedback and time dedicated to this series have made it possible. Without you, it would still sit in a 'saved for later' draft pile. THANK YOU!

And to my readers, thank you for your time. My first book in this series was my first novel and creative challenge. And if you made it to this page, you have literally been part of my author's journey from the start. My deepest gratitude for trusting the process and sticking with me on this ride of creativity.

About the Author

 Kim Malaj lives on a vineyard and homestead in northern Albania with her husband, Arti, author of Northern Albanian Folk Tales, Myths and Legends. Although she is a Show Me State (Missouri) lady at heart, she loves her life at Homestead Albania.

When she's not writing, she tends to the garden, orchard, vineyard, and livestock. She's also been known to brew up batches of raki and wine, and other sweet and savory treats made from the fruits and veggies produced in the garden. She is an avid photographer, an active blogger about the homestead, and a hobbyist drone pilot, learning the art of aerial photography and filming.

Visit the blog: www.HomesteadAlbania.com
For publishing news: www.KimMalaj.com

www.ingramcontent.com/pod-product-compliance
Lightning Source LLC
Chambersburg PA
CBHW010844190726
48286CB00012BA/2978